RED SUNDAY

He was called Dakota, and he had been on the run or in prison for almost a third of his life. When a mysterious stranger breaks him out of Stone Dog Penitentiary, Dakota takes it as an opportunity to walk the straight and narrow – but first he has to repay the favour. Dakota always repaid his debts ... although never before had this involved assassination. As if this isn't enough for one man to deal with there is double-cross and triple-cross, and more flying lead than Dakota has known in all his hell-raising years...

RED SUNDAY

RED SUNDAY

by

Tyler Hatch

Dales Large Print Books
Long Preston, North Yorkshire,
BD23 4ND, England.

British Library Cataloguing in Publication Data.

Hatch, Tyler
    Red Sunday.

    A catalogue record of this book is
    available from the British Library

    ISBN   1-84262-390-7 pbk

First published in Great Britain 2004 by Robert Hale Limited

Copyright © Tyler Hatch 2004

Cover illustration © Faba by arrangement with
Norma Editorial S.A.

Published in Large Print 2005 by arrangement with
Robert Hale Limited

Dales Large Print is an imprint of Library Magna Books Ltd.

Printed and bound in Great Britain by
T.J. (International) Ltd., Cornwall, PL28 8RW

CHAPTER 1

RED SUNDAY

It was the Big Day all over the United States – one hundred years since Independence – the Centennial. Everyone was asked to make it a day that would be remembered for many years to come.

Well, they would sure remember the July 4th celebrations that took place in Stillwater, Texas, that weekend. The man everyone called 'Dakota' could guarantee it. *From now on this day would be remembered as 'Red Sunday'*.

The festivities were hurtling towards the climax of a huge fireworks display along the banks of the Wichita River as Dakota settled down on the pile of sacking beneath the window of the deserted warehouse which faced the lantern-lit area where the barbecue pits glowed. Oxen and hogs roasted, sending off savoury odours that made him salivate even at this distance – a precise 350 yards. A mighty long shot in the fading daylight, but he was up to it, he knew.

If he wasn't, then the rifle was, and all he had to do was draw the bead and caress the trigger – and Judge McManus would know he should never have sent Dakota to the worst prison in Texas for so damned long.

The rifle was a Remington Creedmore built around a precision-made Number 1 rolling block breech-loading system. It was named after the first rifle range in the States, Creed's Farm, Long Island, where, in 1874, a team of six Americans whipped the pants off the all-conquering Irish World Champions. With a thirty-two inch octagonal barrel and chambered for the .44-90 cartridge, a checkered pistol-grip and folding Vernier Peep sight, it was aptly called 'the best breech-loading rifle in the world'.

But its reputation had been gained only in the sports arena – up until now. After today it would be known as the sporting rifle that could drive a ball into human flesh with utter precision. The gun loaded somewhat differently from most breech-loaders. For better accuracy, the cartridge case containing the powder charge was slid into the breech – but the ball, in order to be sized precisely to the barrel, was rammed down the muzzle until it rested against the end of the cartridge. Dakota had already done this; now he laid the rifle down on the soft bag of river sand he was using as a rest for the fore-end, then he crossed the dark room to the board he had loosened two days previously. He took out the Colt .45 six-gun he had hidden there. He checked the loads, took it back to the pile of bags and laid the weapon just within the overlapping burlap. They hadn't wanted him to have any weapon but the Creedmore and, being such a careful man, Dakota didn't care for that restriction.

The Colt might not be needed but there was something queer about this whole deal and he wasn't taking any chances.

Settled again, he was easing the brass horseshoe-shaped butt plate against his shoulder when the first of the river fireworks lit up the darkening water with bursting fountains of various colours and the packed crowds cheered.

Rockets hissed and fizzed and corkscrewed into the sundown sky, exploding with ear-bending cracks, showering red and gold and green and blue sparks. Firecrackers on dangling strings, set up on frames in punts anchored in the river, exploded in volleys that sounded just like a real-life battle between enemy forces.

The pistolshot-like sounds went on and on and the lanterns on the official platform on the river bank showed people moving around – the official party, the hangers-on and organizers, making sure everything went smoothly for the judge when he made his speech and the open-secret announcement that he was running for governor of the state.

There he was! The man himself, being helped up onto his dais, his written speech papers handed to him, steadied by one of the lackeys. His silver hair shone like a halo and then he set his half-moon glasses on the end of his nose and waited – silhouetted plainly against the fire and smoke on the river.

Dakota settled against the special walnut cheek-piece, flipped up the Vernier and set it to the precise 350 yards. Now it all depended on the judge and how he stood – whether he stayed still or decided to move around. But there wasn't much movement he could undertake with safety on the small dais, so the shot would be easy – the sound lost in the rattling volleys of the firecrackers that were burning away on the suspended strings now, leaping from one frame to the next in line.

One frame to go – so he had to draw bead

and make the shot just as the firecrackers began exploding on that last frame.

Like now!

The boom of the Remington was tremendous in the small, closed room and he was thankful he had placed balls of cotton in his ears. He didn't move, finger still holding the trigger back, shoulder registering the kick, his eyes steady.

He was watching Judge McManus, waiting for the suit cloth to erupt as the bullet struck – and then the judge spun violently; there was a large spray of blood and the body crashed off the dais on to the platform.

Utter chaos on the instant.

Dakota reacted by instincts strung as taut as the top strand of a wire fence, rolled away from the table and snatched the six-gun from under the burlap just as the locked door was kicked in and two men burst into the room with blazing guns.

Dakota rolled several times, hearing the bullets splintering the floor. The pile of sacks erupted and toppled over. Sand trickled from the punctured sandbag. The rifle clattered to the floor. And then he flopped onto his belly, the Colt's hammer falling from under his thumb, the gun bucking as he worked the trigger. One of the

11

gunmen staggered, crashed face first into the doorframe, lurched back, gun arm dangling, even as Dakota shifted aim and punched two fast shots into the second man. This gunman flung his arms high, his six-gun flying to crash against the wall. He floundered forward several steps before crashing to the floor.

Dakota came up to one knee, smoking gun swinging to the first man in the doorway who was still falling to his knees. He shot the dying man again, ran to the other and dragged him over to the window amongst the spilled bags. He slumped him into a sitting position in the corner, picked up the Creedmore and hesitated, reluctant to lose such a beautiful weapon, then dumped it in the man's lap across his spread thighs.

The other man he left in the doorway, leapt over him and ran across the landing at the top of the outside stairway where the killers must have been waiting to hear his rifleshot before bursting in to shoot him down in cold blood.

He clattered down the stairs, hearing the strings of firecrackers still punctuating the night with volley-like noise. He could see many people moving on the riverbank about the dais, hear the shouting, none of it making sense to anyone.

Dakota ran down the dark alley, rammed his pistol into his belt. It was no time to be running around with any kind of gun in your hand. He swore when he rounded the end of the alley and saw that the promised getaway horses weren't there. Surprise, surprise!

Goddamn you, Bantry! I knew you were pulling something!

Too late now. He had been double-crossed and there would be no getaway 'arrangements' as promised. He was a clay pigeon, set up neat as you please – a sacrificial lamb.

Only these sons of bitches were going to realize too late that he was a *wolf!*

No time to worry about that now. He had to get out of town and mighty damn fast. If that Stillwater sheriff – what was his name? *Doolin.* Yeah, if that Doolin had been down by the river near the speech platform – and he would have been, *should* have been – then he would organize things pronto. Close off the town's perimeters, bottle him up.

God-damn! Why had he let Bantry talk him into it? Hell, he knew why: he was a man who always paid his debts, was Dakota, *always*, and he owed Bantry for breaking him out of that corner of hell they called the

13

Cesspit. That wasn't its official name, of course, but it was more appropriate.

Someone called out and he stopped running instinctively, crouching against the clapboard wall of a store.

'Yeah, you! What the hell's your goddamn hurry!'

A medium-tall man was coming towards him and he glimpsed the outline of a shotgun even as the last of the firecrackers down by the river gave out. Dakota stayed in the shadow as much as possible and lifted his hands.

'Easy, Deputy! Easy! I seen someone run outta that freighter's warehouse and he had a gun in his hand. Looked kinda suspicious and I was lookin' for him... You see him come this way?'

'No. Now let's take a look at you, Mr Good Citizen, who thinks nothin' of riskin' his life!'

'I was just hurryin' to get to the river to hear the Judge's speech when I seen him fall and all hell seemed to break loose. There was gunfire in that warehouse and this feller come runnin' out and I... What the hell happened at the river, anyway?'

The deputy was close enough to poke him with the shotgun now and Dakota grunted,

14

doubled up, still managing to hide his face. The lawman growled something and stepped close to grab Dakota's collar and pull him upright.

Dakota came with a speed that lifted him onto his toes. As he did so he grabbed the shotgun, yanked it out of the hands of the startled deputy. The man was good, though, quick as a snake, jumping back and slapping a hand to his six-gun butt. But Dakota swung the long-barrelled Greener, catching him across the side of the head. The deputy gasped as his legs buckled. Dakota slammed him with the brass-bound butt of the shotgun and the man stretched out.

The Greener was a fine weapon but this was no night to be seen carrying a long-gun, so Dakota broke it open, tossed away the shells, then quickly unbuckled the unconscious lawman's gun rig and put it around his own waist. The belt only just fitted but he felt better with a firearm and spare ammunition.

He ran on through the dark streets, hearing a lot of shouting and what sounded like wailing. The river was only reflecting the lanternlight now. Someone had stopped the infernal racket of swooshing rockets and exploding firecrackers. Dakota was looking

15

back and stumbled off the end of a low dock at the ferry landing. The river was low and he didn't fall into the water, but the ground was soggy. He sloshed through the shallows and made for a skiff he could just make out tied to the bank. His elation was soon dashed when he saw that there was no oar and the boat was chained to a heavy stake driven into the ground.

His luck was deserting him, he thought, already moving away from the river. Just as well, too, for he heard oars and knew that that damn Doolin had already put men on the river, searching....

Horses whinnied and hoofs clattered to his left. He knew there would be men guarding the bridge over Whistler's Creek, which ran into the main river. He swung the other way, went to ground as a band of men rode past at the end of the side street where he was. He cursed, guessing where they were going.

To bottle up the trail out to the ranches, cutting yet another avenue of escape. That left only two more directions he could take to get out of town −and he had to get a horse yet. He knew blamed well Doolin would have the livery covered, and all the hitching racks on Main.

It would be just a matter of time now when they would close the net and capture him.

He wished he knew the town better but there hadn't been time to get oriented and, anyway, he couldn't have shown his face around here for fear of recognition. Bantry had told him there were wanted dodgers everywhere with his likeness on them.

More riders and voices this time. *That Doolin, curse the man! He was just too good a lawman! He had armed men already searching the streets!*

Well, the answer was simple enough: he had to get off the streets before they saw him. Problem was, where to go...? Most places were locked up tight because everyone was out at the river for the celebrations.

He came into a yard through a tumbledown fence and made his way towards the dark shape of a building fronting the side street. He didn't know what the place was. It looked like someone's house but there had been an extension tacked on the back. Desperate, listening for sounds of riders or men afoot, he crept up towards the black shape, felt his way along the clapboard walls, getting a whiff of some vaguely familiar but unpleasant smell – sweetish, yet pungent, tickling his nostrils. He banged into a door unexpectedly, put out a hand to steady himself – and felt a latch give under his touch.

An unlocked door!

His luck had returned and he opened it part-way, gun in his free hand. The door was heavier and thicker than usual, he thought, frowning. He waited. Nothing happened and he stepped inside quickly, closing the door after him, easing the latch down. It seemed a lot cooler in here than outside.

By God! The smell was much worse in here, too. His eyes were watering. He wanted to cough but fought to stifle the reflex, groped his way around the pitch-dark room. His hand touched a trestle of some kind and at the same time he smelled wood-shavings. A better smell than the other but...

'Jesus!'

He jumped back as the word exploded from him. His groping hand had touched a human face: *someone was sleeping in here...*

He swallowed. No! This face was dead cold, waxy. He felt his heart lurch. *Yeah, this man was sleeping, all right. Sleeping the sleep from which he would never awake.*

He had stumbled into an undertaker's parlour.

CHAPTER 2

DEAD MAN'S RIDE

Cleeve Overholser was Stillwater's official undertaker. Now he opened the door of his funeral parlour's cold room, stood aside to allow entry of the two sweating men carrying the door with a horse blanket covering the body resting on it.

He held the thick door back with one hand. The light of the square lantern in his other lighted the way for the men. They made their way to two empty trestles and slid their door across them. A third man pushed past Overholser and the light glinted from the metal star pinned to his shirt.

Sheriff Linus Doolin turned to the undertaker as the man closed the heavy door.

'Get some more light in here, Cleeve.'

Without hurry, fat Cleeve Overholser waddled over to where a bank of three more square lanterns stood and lit each one. He nodded to the two townsmen who hung them from hooks against the wall. The light showed a stack of finished and half-finished coffins and also one, polished, resting on a pair of trestles, looking ready for transfer to the grave.

'Who's in there?' asked Doolin in that clipped, abrupt manner he had, pointing to the coffin.

'Chuck Darcy. Dianna's s'posed to be pickin' him up after the celebrations and takin' him back to the ranch.'

'Why ain't she havin' him buried in the town cemetery?'

'Ask her. Got some bee in her bonnet, had words with Preacher Hallum. I heard she doesn't think he can give Chuck a proper service.'

'Well, he better sober up and polish his sermons or whatever, when it comes time to bury the judge!' Doolin growled. 'Judge McManus was a mighty good friend to this town, was born here – which is why he chose it to announce that he was standin' for governor. His family'll want it done proper and that means you better do your part and make a damn fine job of it, Cleeve!'

'I always do a damn fine job.' Cleeve wheezed as he tossed aside the horse blanket and looked down at the body of McManus.

'Got him through the left temple. See what the pressure caused by the bullet can do to the face? Wouldn't recognize the old judge, would you? Popped his eyes outta their sockets. I peel this here flap back you can see part of his brain, pull it down further and there's his upper teeth–Why, where you goin', boys? What's your hurry? Don't you want to stay and watch me drain the judge's body fluids and flush him out with formalin, take out his organs and...? Well, will you look at that! Gone like the goddamn Apaches was on their tails.'

He turned to Doolin, chuckling, but soon sobered when he saw the sheriff's stern face.

'I oughta slap you out from between your damn ears, Cleeve! You ain't funny. You ain't even amusin'... An' you oughta have more respect for a man like the judge. He put plenty of business your way when he was hangin' outlaws all over Wichita County.'

Overholser shrugged his fat shoulders.

'Just figured it'd be fun to stir up them two roustabouts. You see the colour of their faces? Pea-green!' He made himself look sombre. 'But, if you want, I'll take a more "grave" view of things, Linus!'

'Forget about bein' a comedian, Cleeve.

You do a damn fine job on McManus. I got respect for the man and his family. You make him look like he's at peace and just like they'd remember him in life.'

'Christ, Linus, no one can do that! Just *look* at him! He's a goddamn mess and it'll cost a fortune to rebuild that into a face. Why, I'd be as well to slap dumplin' dough over it and thumb in a couple raisins for eyes – Hey!'

Doolin took one long step forward, fisted up the undertaker's shirt front and shook the man. Cleeve's blubbery face went all shapeless and his belly quivered. He gasped as Doolin's pistol rammed between his eyes.

'*Shut up!* You quit that damn talk or I'll stuff you into one of your own coffins and bury you alive! I told you what you have to do! Now you *do* it!' He flung the undertaker half way across the room. The man grabbed at the coffin containing Chuck Darcy. It started to fall off the trestle stand. Doolin was fast enough to grab the end and keep it from toppling to the floor. The two men struggled to get it back onto the stand.

'Didn't realize young Chuck was so damn heavy!' panted Doolin, still glaring at Cleeve. 'You gonna gimme any more trouble?'

Overholser shook his head, gasping for

breath, face a dark, unhealthy red.

'I – I'll do my best, Linus!'

'You better! Now Mrs McManus and her daughter will likely expect to view the body sometime tomorrow mornin'. You have him ready.'

'Hell, I'll have to work on him all night!'

'So, work on him all night.'

'Who's gonna pay? You don't seem to realize just how much has to be done...'

'Just do it, Cleeve. We'll worry about payment afterwards.'

The undertaker snorted as Doolin went out and closed the thick door after him.

'You mean *I*'ll have to worry about payment afterwards, you damn bully!'

Still muttering he took off his jacket, and rolled up his sleeves and went to a dark corner. There were several clattering sounds as he gathered up his equipment: rubber gloves, tubes and metal joiners, hand pumps and one foot pump, a large glass carboy of formaldehyde, and a set of evil-looking eviscerating tools, the short knives with curved blades and slender steel rods with hooks on the ends, of varying lengths and diameters.

He set the instruments on a bench near the trestles and stripped off McManus's clothes.

'Hel-lo!' he said aloud, bending over the man suddenly. 'My, my. You been shot twice, Judge, ol' man! One through the temple which did for you good an' proper, but you got a bullet-graze on the tip of your right shoulder, too. Now I wonder what Mr Marvellous Doolin would make of that?'

He peered more closely at the shallow groove cut in the tip of the white shoulder.

'Hmmmm. Goes from back to front. Now ain't that queer? Fatal shot from the left, a harmless one on the right, but coming from *behind?*'

He spun as he heard the street door open. *Blast! He didn't want any interruptions now!*

A girl entered. She was dressed in a checked shirt, with leather chaps over denim work-trousers. A narrow-brimmed hat was perched on the back of her head, light danced from highlights in her raven hair and also from somewhere deep in her dark eyes. She strode right up to Cleeve Overholser, glanced briefly at the dead judge and grimaced involuntarily at the judge's face and the terrible instruments on the roll of rawhide which Cleeve had spread out.

'I've come for Chuck,' she said, wrenching her eyes towards the fat undertaker. 'I'm taking him home with me tonight.'

'It's not the wisest thing to do, Dianna. Hallum will pull himself together and deliver a fine eulogy and burial service, I'm sure. Just give him little time.'

'I intend to bury my brother myself on Double D land, Cleeve. It's where he ought to be even if he did spend more time in town lately – thanks to that whore who not only bled him of every cent he had but provoked him into challenging Roy Callahan to a gunfight he must've known he couldn't win.' Her voice trembled as she said the words. 'I'll have to owe you for the coffin and whatever – work – you had to do on him, Cleeve.'

'Nothing but a little rouge and eye make-up, Dianna. The shot didn't – mutilate him any. You want to see him...?'

She hesitated very briefly then shook her head.

'No. I prefer to remember him as I last saw him, laughing and waving as he rode away – happy.'

She was showing signs of distress now and Cleeve wasn't so insensitive that he didn't notice. He wiped his hands on a grubby towel and touched her arm.

'I'll lend you a hand to load the coffin if

you care to bring your buckboard around. I intended to screw a brass cross onto the lid, but...' he gestured towards the judge's body, 'Doolin wants him prepared for family viewing by the morning ... and it's going to be a long job.'

'Thank you, Cleeve.' She looked steadily at McManus now. 'It seems a terrible way for anyone to die, but I'm afraid I feel nothing for Judge McManus or his family. He treated my father badly when he was alive and we lost half our ranch because of his decisions in favour of Lang Bantry. The man who killed him was a murderer and a cowardly one at that, but I wouldn't mind shaking his hand.'

'Hush, girl! Don't talk like that! McManus had a lot of friends in this town... You have your buckboard handy?'

'Yes – I'll bring it. Thank you for the thought of the cross, Cleeve. Chuck was not religious but it was nice of you.'

She went out and he turned to the coffin on the stand, giving the lid a little shake. It had a wooden lip that overlapped the casket itself, holding it so it couldn't slide off, and there were eight ready-drilled screw holes in the edge of the top.

'Well, if she don't want to look at you

again, Chuck, I might's well seal you in.' He reached for a bag of screws and a driver, but scratched his head, frowning a little as he saw a smear of wood-dust around each of the holes, showing against the single coat of polish he had given the lid.

'That's odd. You know, I *thought* I'd screwed that lid on earlier, but what with all the hurry to get to the celebrations and so on...' He sighed and shook his head as he thumbed in the first screw and began to drive it home. 'You're gettin' old, Cleeve. Too much to do. You're gonna have to write out a schedule and cross off the jobs as you do 'em ... or else hire an assistant, God forbid! I make little enough as it is.'

Then he heard the clatter as the girl drove her buckboard towards the door of the cold room and Sheriff Doolin's voice telling her to watch out for that damn assassin on her way home – he could be anywhere.

'I think we got him bottled-up in town, but cain't be sure. You take care, Dianna, hear?'

'Thank you, Linus – I'll be careful...'

Overholser quickly drove a screw into each corner of the lid, fumbling, splintering one edge a little. He swore.

'That'll hold it till she gets home. She can

put the extra ones in if she wants. I just have to get on with fixin' up the judge or Doolin'll kill me!'

In his hurry, one of the screws missed the edge and didn't bite into the coffin properly but he didn't notice, or, if he did, couldn't spare the time to set it right.

'Be right with you, Dianna,' he called, panting. 'And the quicker she gets outta here the quicker I can get back to the judge – may he squirm in hell!'

Then, as an afterthought, adding: 'And Linus Doolin, too!'

But he almost whispered that last part, looking around him a little fearfully, half-expecting to see the sheriff coming through the door.

Someone had found the deputy whom Dakota had slugged during his getaway from the warehouse.

Doolin looked down at the unconscious man, half-dried blood from the wound caking in the left eye, his mouth hanging slackly. The sheriff swore.

'Trust Torres to get himself into trouble. Wonder who done it to him? No, forget about that – take him to a sawbones and then get on with the search.'

'We got Magill and Sawyer lookin' through the buildin's over yonder, Linus,' one of the men said, gesturing. 'Them warehouses an' stores have all been closed for the day–'

'Judas priest, you're wastin' time!' Doolin snapped. 'The judge was shot in the left temple, the *left* temple. Anyone who tried to shoot him from here would have to be usin' a gun with a right-angled barrel! Chrissakes, use your heads! There's nothin' in this part. Get over to River Street and the Mex section. That's where we'll find somethin' if we're gonna find anythin' at all. We've got the town bottled-up tighter'n a whore's purse. Son of a bitch can't get out, so *run him down!* And I mean now!'

The men murmured and ducked their heads, two carrying off the unconscious deputy between them, his boots dragging. Then just as Doolin, feeling – and looking – a mite frantic, started to swing away, a voice called from one of the dark warehouse buildings.

'Sheriff! Linus – better get up here! I think we've found the killer. But someone else found him before we did!'

Doolin sprinted across, the other men hesitating, wanting to know what Magill had found before moving on to continue their own search along River Street.

Upstairs, where Sawyer had found a lamp and fired it up, Doolin thumbed back his hat, exposing his long hatchet face, as he looked down at one dead man with three bullets in him, and a second corpse, with a fancy-looking rifle beside him, with two wounds in his chest, a six-gun on the floor beside one curled-under leg.

Sawyer, middle-aged, sloppy, shirt tails hanging out, grinned, showing worn and yellowed teeth. He made a grand gesture with his arm.

'Da-daaaaa! There we are, Linus – mystery solved. Bushwhacker took his shot from that there window, this here cowpoke for some reason heard him and busted in and they shot it out, killin' each other.' He stooped and picked up the Remington Creedmore rifle, almost caressing the oiled walnut stock. 'Fancy gun, used specially for the job, I'd reckon... Single-shot, rollin'-block breech, twin triggers, one for takin' up slack, Vernier scale peep-sight... Man, reckon this woulda cost a couple hundred bucks, five times as much as the run-of-the-mill Winchester lever action.'

Doolin took the weapon and examined it,

Magill holding the lamp closer for him. *Damn, but this was sure some fancy murder weapon!* But he knew it wasn't. Anyone with half a brain would know that. He ran his hand down the blued octagonal barrel and looked Sawyer straight in the eye as he observed:

'Barrel don't have a bend in it.'

Sawyer blinked and Magill, too, looked puzzled.

Doolin added in a hard, flat voice: 'Because that's what it would need to put a bullet in Judge McManus's head *from the left hand side!*'

Sawyer frowned, looked from the gun to the sheriff and then to the dead man sprawled beneath the window.

'But ... this here feller's a stranger. He's got the look of bein' a wild-ass, Linus!'

'He's not only a wild-ass, he has to be a magician to have killed the judge from here...'

'Then what's this all about? I mean, it's plain there was a gunfight and... Hell, beats me!'

'I'll take this gun and we'll look into it later. I dunno what happened here, but McManus wasn't shot from this angle, I guarantee that. Better tell Cleeve to come collect these fellers when he's got time. Then go on over to River Street and the Quarter and help with the search there. We've gotta flush that bastard pronto! I want him in my jail by sun-up!'

Doolin didn't get his wish.

First, Doc Halloran sent word that Deputy Torres had regained consciousness and wanted to see the sheriff.

The slim deputy looked mighty sick and sorry when Doolin found him sitting on the edge of a bed in Gold's infirmary, head bandaged, gaunt and grey-faced.

'What you want, Pete?' Doolin asked impatiently as he came in, not even thinking to ask how the man was feeling, his face all bruised and misshapen. 'We're still searchin' and—'

'I seen him, Linus. Seen him and tangled with the son of a bitch – he clobbered me with my own shotgun.'

Doolin stiffened and sat down on the bed beside Torres, listening in silence as the deputy told him of his encounter with Dakota.

'I'm sure it was him, Linus. He was runnin' from somethin' and he had a six-gun an' he sure didn't waste any time sluggin' me.'

'You must've gotten too close for him to grab your Greener!' Doolin said unsympathetically. 'See his face?'

'Just a flash.' Torres paused, seemed a little reluctant to continue, but at Doolin's frown said: 'I think it was that escaped prisoner – Dakota.'

Doolin jumped to his feet. 'Christ! I knew it! Someone who had it in for the judge! But what the hell was he doin' over near the freight warehouses?'

Doolin explained about the judge having been shot in the left temple.

'He couldn't've shot him from over in that section of town, even though it gave a good outlook on the river where the fireworks were.'

'Well, I could be mistaken about who it was, but I still say that feller, *whoever* he was, had been up to no good.'

'Yeah,' Doolin said slowly, thinking about the dead men in the warehouse. 'But just what the hell was it...'

They both jerked their heads up, Torres grabbing his quickly and moaning, as they heard someone calling the sheriff's name wildly.

'Linus! Linus! Where the hell are you?'

Doolin swore softly. 'Cleeve Overholser!

Judas, what now?' He raised his voice. 'In the infirmary, Cleeve. What the hell's the matter?'

Fat Cleeve Overholser staggered in, panting sweating, still with his bloody, stained work-apron on, still wearing his elbow-length rubber gloves, reeking of formaldehyde and other unpleasant odours. He leaned against the door-jamb, ignoring the doctor who came hurrying in demanding that Cleeve should lower his voice.

'This is an infirmary, for God's sake!'

Cleeve nodded but kept looking wide-eyed at Doolin as his mouth worked. Eventually he could speak.

'The judge – big man...' He spread his hands, flapping his arms briefly like a dying bird. 'Shoulders... Wasn't sure I had a – a coffin made that was – wide enough... Looked through – stack in the corner... One fell. Lid came off an' – an' a body rolled out...'

Doolin frowned. 'Body in a coffin in an undertakin' parlour – sounds pretty much what you'd expect, Cleeve.' There was heavy sarcasm in his voice.

Cleeve narrowed his eyes. 'Oh? You think so, huh? Well, not this body. It was Chuck Darcy!'

34

The silent, suffering Deputy Torres frowned a little and looked from Doolin to the undertaker. The sheriff was frowning, deeply.

'Thought Dianna collected him? I seen her backin'-up her buckboard to your cold room, earlier...'

Cleeve swallowed, nodded. 'Helped her load up myself.'

'Then what the hell is Chuck's body doin' in another coffin? You give her the wrong one?'

Cleeve shook his head vehemently. 'Only had one ready-polished. Did it specially for her and put Chuck in myself, screwed down the lid. And goin' by the weight there was a body in that coffin when we loaded it onto Dianna's buckboard.'

'Then who the hell was it?' demanded Doolin, trying not to let what he was thinking crowd into the front of his mind. *'Who the hell was in that coffin, Cleeve?'*

'I kinda thought you might like to answer that question yourself, Linus. Me, I reckon there's only one man it could've been – an' I don't think he was quite ready for buryin'.'

CHAPTER 3

DEAD MAN STANDING

Dianna Darcy couldn't sleep – not with Chuck's body still outside in the back of the buckboard in the barn where she had unhitched it last night.

She was too tired after the long drive through the darkness, knowing what load she was carrying, biting back the sobs and fighting the tears that kept oozing down her face despite her efforts.

Chuck had been a good brother, younger than her by almost three years, and, accordingly, a little wild. But, essentially, he had been a good man. Until he met that whore, of course... Well, she had seen other young men in and around Stillwater and how they behaved when the sap started to flow and the basic urges of the human race roared through their systems. She didn't begrudge Chuck his curiosity and experiences with women, but that whore was just too much. She didn't know what the woman had in mind, whether she thought Chuck came from a rich family and she could somehow latch onto a share of the money, or simply that it pleased her to have such control over a strong young man like Chuck Darcy. Whatever it was, it was fatal for Chuck.

For whatever reason, the whore played Chuck against Roy Callahan, a notorious, trigger-happy hardcase about town who had six notches on the butts of his flashy six-guns. Somehow she had convinced Chuck that Callahan had insulted her or harmed her in some way and Chuck, being the decent man he was, set out to put things to right. Of course, you didn't reason with men like Roy Callahan. The man relished any sort of confrontation because they always ended the one way – in a shoot-out. To date he had always been the one to walk away.

Sheriff Doolin claimed his hands were tied.

'Sorry, Dianna, but there're a couple dozen witnesses to swear Chuck started things, reached for his gun first. I cain't very well lock a man away for protectin' hisself.'

'You know Callahan manipulated Chuck, provoked him into going for his gun! You *know* it, Sheriff! He's done it before to other men.'

Doolin had shaken his head slowly. 'I have to go by the written law, Dianna, and this is a clear case of self-defence. I'm sorry.'

Well, someone was going to be sorry, she told herself for the hundredth time. Then, bracing herself, she went out to the barn. Avoiding looking at the buckboard in the shadows she reached for the pick and long-handled shovel. She would bury Chuck under that cottonwood above the creek. He had always liked to sit there and play his harmonica in the evening and have a last cigarette before turning in.

The emotions were swirling within her and she choked them back. She rested the tools against the gapped wall of the barn and walked across to the buckboard.

She wiped her palms down her denim trousers and approached the side of the vehicle, not knowing exactly what she was going to do, but somehow wanting to be as close as possible to her dead brother. After all, in an hour or so he would be six feet under the ground and she would – would – never...

'*Oh, my God!*'

The wailing exclamation escaped from her with a rush. She felt her eyes widen; then there was some kind of storm in her brain.

She grabbed at the buckboard, felt her legs giving away as the barn and everything tilted wildly and swirled around her before she collapsed on the straw-littered ground, half-beneath the vehicle.

The barn was already warm with the sun and a few flies and a curious hornet buzzed. Dust motes floated lazily.

Then something moved way back in the shadows at the rear of the building and Dakota stepped out, six-gun down at his side. His clothes were dark with sweat, clinging to his body, and his hair was damp and matted. He looked at the unconscious girl, muttered a soft curse, and moved towards the door. Now would be the perfect time to rope a horse in the corral, saddle up and vamoose....

But he paused, teeth tugging at his bottom lip as he frowned. He sighed, and went back and knelt beside her. He rolled her onto her back, lightly slapped her pale face.

'C'mon! Wake up! C'mon, now! You'll be OK in a minute...' His heart was pounding. *Christ, get the hell out of here, you blamed fool! So it was a hell of a shock for her to find the empty coffin and the splintered lid where you'd finally kicked it off almost at the point where you had resigned yourself to suffocating...*

'What the hell am I doing?' he asked out loud, looking around him. Since when had he felt sorry for people? But there was something about this girl. Lying in the coffin on the trestles in the undertaking parlour, the lid not screwed down at that stage, he had heard her opinion of Judge McManus and she had also seemed hostile to Doolin.

Let's be honest about this: was he concerned about the girl because she'd fainted, had such a shock, or was he subconsciously figuring that here was one person who might help him get away before Doolin arrived? And arrive the damn sheriff would. Her brother's body would be discovered quickly enough and it wouldn't take Doolin any time at all to figure out who had ridden out of town in Chuck's coffin in the back of the buckboard.

He had just decided he would go saddle a mount when the girl stirred and moaned and tried to sit up. She fell sideways; he grabbed her and she snapped her head around, focusing instantly as surprise took her. She stared for one wild instant, then pushed him away and slid backwards on her buttocks, almost beneath the buckboard now.

'Who – wh – wha– Who the blazes are you?'

'That don't matter. Are you OK now?'

She blinked and ran a small hand across her forehead, frowning. Then she froze, her eyes going up towards the floor of the vehicle.

'My God! Chuck...! Oh! What's happened...? What've you done with my brother?'

'Look, I'm sorry, Miss Darcy...'

'How d'you know my name?'

'Well, I heard it – when I was lying in the coffin, before that fat undertaker screwed the lid down...'

She was backing away again, trying to rise. He reached to help her but she slapped his arm away, quickly rolled and came to her feet on the far side of the buckboard.

Dakota straightened and let out a startled yell as a rusty reaping-hook sailed past his head. Then as he straightened, she charged around the rear of the buckboard, lunging at him with a pitchfork. He stumbled and fell and the tines thudded into the weather-grey wood of the buckboard, stuck there as she struggled to free them. It gave him time to roll to his feet but she jarred backwards as the tines jerked free, spun and jabbed at him.

He sucked in his belly with a hiss and threw

up his arms as she forced him back into a corner, his feet tangling with discarded tools lying around. They clattered as he shouted, thoroughly alarmed now:

'Hold it, you crazy woman!'

She spoke, forcing the words between her teeth, eyes blazing.

'What – did – you – do – with – my – brother?'

'I put him in another coffin, stacked empty ones on top. Look, I'm sorry, but Doolin had me cornered. I couldn't get out of that damn undertaker's so I took a chance and climbed into that coffin. I couldn't fix the lid from the inside, of course, and I was worried the fat man would notice, but apparently he didn't, just put in fresh screws.' He grimaced. 'I was really worried then. There wasn't much air, but one of the screws hadn't gone into the coffin properly and the lid's corner was raised a little. Even so, it took me most of the night to kick my way out. I was trying not to make any noise that would alarm you...'

'D'you think I believe in ghosts...?'

'I dunno – I just thought you were likely upset enough without hearing sounds coming from the coffin.'

She frowned briefly, surprised at his

words. 'I ought to skewer you like a fish on a hook!'

'I really am sorry, miss. It's a terrible thing to happen to you but I was pretty damn desperate.'

'You're the one, aren't you? The one who killed Judge McManus?'

He said nothing for a long moment and then spoke very carefully.

'I aimed to clip his right shoulder only. I didn't try to kill him. I don't know what went wrong.'

She studied him. 'It sounds stupid, what you just said. Why do I find myself trying to decide whether I believe you?'

He felt a little surge of hope. 'I'm telling the truth. Look, I was hired to just graze the judge's shoulder so the sound of the shot would be lost in the noise of the fireworks. I could tell by the way he went down that he'd been shot in the head.' He paused, stared levelly at her. 'I'm just not that bad a shot. It had to be the rifle, although it was a Remington Creedmore, just about the most accurate rifle in the country, if not the whole damn world at this time...'

'Who on earth would hire someone to just wound the judge?' It was plain from her tone that she didn't believe him.

'It's a long story, but basically it was to show him just how easy it would be for an assassin to kill him – so he would beef-up his protection. Seems he scoffed at the idea that anyone would want him dead. But now...' He shrugged.

'It still sounds queer to me. Why couldn't whoever hired you just *tell* him he was taking risks?'

'Seems he was warned plenty. Putting on a front, I suppose. Anyway, McManus is dead now, isn't he?'

'Ye-es.' She seemed slightly distracted, as if she was thinking of something else. 'Did you say you were aiming at his right shoulder?'

'The bullet was supposed to just graze him.'

'Someone must have had a lot of faith in your shooting!' The scepticism was back but there was a strange look on her face which he couldn't quite decipher.

'I used to do OK at target shoots, won a lot of trophies, worked with refining guns, to make them more accurate. Had a small reputation for it. But it was a long time ago. I must've been a lot more rusty than I figured.'

She was silent and he eased his weight

from one foot to the other, but she immediately thrust the fork tines an inch closer to let him know she was still alert.

'I – saw Judge McManus's body at the undertaker's,' she said slowly. 'I don't think you killed him at all.'

Dakota stiffened. 'He was only wounded then...?'

'No, I don't mean that – he's dead all right. But although I tried not to look at him I did see the wound in his head. It was... awful, what it had done to him.' She took a deep breath, looked him straight in the eye. 'The bullet had entered his left temple.'

Dakota stared, frowning, shook his head.

'Impossible! That gun couldn't possibly shoot like that from the position I was in! I thought it might've pulled to the left and the bullet took him in the back of the head, but it *can't* have entered by the left *temple*. The damn gun would have to shoot around corners!'

She watched him, saw the genuine shock and puzzlement there on his face. Then she said slowly:

'Unless there was a second gun that fired the same time as you did – from somewhere on the judge's left.'

CHAPTER 4

STONE DOG

That was the answer, of course!

He'd known it as soon as he saw Mc-Manus collapse in that crumbling, boneless way a man does when his vital life functions have been snuffed out instantly. He had not only *known* it, but he had suspected all along that Bantry would pull something like this.

It had been all too easy, too glib, right up until the time he had stretched out in that empty freight warehouse and squeezed the trigger...

Then why did you fall for it, you stupid bastard?

Well, what *could* you do when a man who'd just busted you out of three long years of hell – with at least another seven years staring you in the face – asked you to do him one small favour? You could have said, 'no', but that likely would have earned you a bullet. In any case, you had always paid your debts and you had been wondering how in hell you were going to pay back Lang Bantry, a complete stranger, who had gotten you out of that prison – at no small cost to himself. You'd known all along that men had died during that break-out and that it would have to be all squared away sometime – and at high cost. It only made sense.

I mean, think about it for a minute... Think about what must've been involved to get you all the way from the Sinkhole in Stone Dog Penitentiary to here and now...

McManus had put him in Stone Dog. Not because he had beaten Charley Page half to death and wrecked the best saloon bar west of the Pecos in the process, but because he happened to be proving-up on land that friends of McManus coveted.

Later, he had worked it out that that was why Page, a bully and maimer of men, had been sicced onto him. It had been a gamble: Page might have beaten him to a pulp as he had so many men before but someone either sensed or knew that the man called Dakota was no ordinary nester or sod-buster. They might even have known he was a man trying to push his past over the nearest cliff so he could make a new start. He had thrown away those guns he had notched like a damn flashy kid over the years. What had it been...? Eleven? Twelve notches? Yeah, twelve. Every gunfight deliberately provoked.

But there were other men who had died under those guns whose deaths he hadn't notched for recalling any time he felt like it. The men he had hired out to kill in range wars or others who had resisted when he, in company, had held up a payroll stage or robbed a bank. He hadn't kept tally of those men.

He had only wanted to notch his guns for those he had challenged or who had challenged him – and lost. *Big shot!*

One morning he had wakened in his lonely camp in the high country of the Warbonnets, breaking the ice in the stream so as to fill the coffee pot, and it had hit him like an arrow out of ambush.

This was one helluva life he was leading and it was getting him nowhere. Fast.

That last gunfight had seen him toting a bullet in his side and the dead man's brothers had put two more in his back. He was lucky to be alive. There were other men hunting him up here in this frontier land, too, some for revenge, some for the bounty on his head.

You're plumb loco! You ought to get the hell out of this, away from this northern cold, make a fresh start...

So he had headed for Texas and some sunshine. He was making a fair fist of proving-up on his river-bottom land, when those sons of bitches who, he had later found out, were friends of Judge McManus, made their move. They made him an offer at first, and it was a fair one, but he simply didn't want to sell. So they tried to run him off, rousted his herds, beat up the two drifters he had hired, pulled down his fences. He had fought back. Then they turned Charley Page loose on him and McManus finished the job for them...

The judge made damn sure he wouldn't be back for a long time, too. When McManus had learned he couldn't pay for the damages done, he had used it as an excuse to bring down a longer sentence – five years. Dakota had exploded in that court room at such an unfair punishment, slugged two of the court's guards and had almost made it across McManus's bench, his hands reaching for the fat throat, before they had subdued him.

He had regained consciousness to find out he had been sentenced to a minimum of ten years' hard on the Stone Dog chaingangs of west Texas. The worst prison in the United States, where few lived to serve out their full sentences and most left only by way of the undertaker's wagon.

'You're a dead man, McManus! I'll live through this and I'll get out – and I'll come for you and blow your head off your shoulders!'

Those threatening words earned him even more inhuman treatment in a place notorious for its inhumanity.

Three long, hard years. Two attempts on his life – no explanation, but none was needed in that hell-hole: a man could die in a hundred ways simply by looking sideways at another inmate who was in a killing mood. The brutal guards had had orders to treat men whose names were on a special list more harshly than the other prisoners. Dakota's name was up near the top of that list and he knew it had to have been McManus who put it there. They aimed to break his spirit so that he would either die inside the walls of Stone Dog or, *if or when* he should be released, he would have no inclination to carry out his death threat to Judge McManus.

At first he raged and fought them all – prisoners, guards, a loner, hated or feared by all. He earned himself a record amount of time in the Sinkhole, a stinking well-like place just below the drainage system outlets, deep in filth and slops. Garbage was emptied each night through a wide-grilled cover. Prisoners on the special list were sentenced to hours, days or weeks in the Sinkhole. The record was seventeen days – held by Dakota. He was more dead than alive when they hauled him out. He had had to spend time in the prison infirmary, much to the chagrin of the warden, but the man had been ordered to care for Dakota by a visiting committee of do-gooders who had arrived unannounced just as they were preparing Dakota for yet another week in the Sinkhole.

It was while he was receiving medical treatment for the many infected sores and the terrible fevers which racked him that he was first contacted by one of Bantry's lackeys.

The trusty who doubled as orderly in the infirmary slipped him a note. It was brief and to the point: *If you want to get out of Stone Dog, just tell the orderly.*

No signature, of course, and when he had told the trusty 'OK', then asked who sent it, the man pulled back quickly from Dakota's grip.

'Can't tell you a thing. I just pass it on, do what I'm told – and you better, too!'

Nothing happened. After two weeks he went back to the chaingang and, perhaps because of the note, Dakota behaved, followed orders, took the odd cuff and kick without reaction. The guards grinned crookedly.

'Boys, I do believe we is finally seein' a leeeeetle bend in good ol' Dakota's spirit!' crowed the head guard. 'I think he has finally seen the light!'

That was what Dakota wanted them to think as he waited impatiently for some further contact from the man who had written that note. The trusty had met with a fatal 'accident', he learned, so there was nothing he could find out from that source. Whenever someone approached him he waited tensely: was this it? Was this the one who would deliver the word, telling him how and when he would get out of this living hell?

It was five weeks after leaving the infirmary that it happened. He was working with a gang, clearing brush for a new road for a stageline that would be running through this part of Texas come the fall. When they reached a boulder-studded hillside, the explosives experts were called in and huge boulders were blasted loose. The shattered rock was moved by the convicts, some of it to be reduced to rubble that would eventually act as a roadbed.

On a scorching day, when the heat waves curled up from the earth and rocks and the guards' horses stood with sagging heads in the scant shade of a lonely clump of trees, the dynamite men arrived to blast down a house-size boulder part-way up the slope. Some of the prisoners figured it was too high above the level of the road to matter but they weren't averse to taking a short break while the charges were set and the fuses cut and laid out.

Then one of the guards, mounted, walked his horse in amongst the reclining prisoners in their leg-irons, trampling some but ignoring their protests. He pointed his quirt at Dakota who was half-sprawled near a scraggy tree, watching alertly as the guard approached.

'You! Dakota! Come with me.'

Dakota stood, shrugging as the men around him looked questions at him. He shuffled forward, holding the slack of his leg chains awkwardly so that he was bent almost double. The guard's quirt slashed across his shoulders.

'Hurry it up, damn you!'

The fuses were already burning and the dynamite men were running for cover: if any of the prisoners noticed they ran *around* the bulge of the hill instead of placing themselves near the convicts, no one said anything. Not out loud, leastways.

'For Chrissakes, *hurry!*' growled the mounted guard and he leaned down, grabbed a handful of Dakota's grimy uniform shirt and half-lifted the man across the saddle. He spurred away and Dakota struggled to stay upright, his feet running and flailing one moment, free of the ground the next, and still in motion, slapped down again, wrenching his body as he twisted and flailed in an attempt to stay upright.

The soiled jacket was twisted tight around his throat and he was gasping, slowly strangling, futilely beating at the guard with one hand, hanging on desperately with the other. The horse jerked and snorted with each new rake of the guard's spurs or slash of the quirt. And then they were around the hill and Dakota glimpsed the explosives men huddled together behind a row of boulders.

As he wondered what the hell they were

doing there, the world seemed to shake and he felt the tremor through his body and clear up into his back teeth, ear-drums bending. He fell, hands reaching out ahead, dragging air down into his burning lungs, dodging and rolling away from the flying hoofs of the horse, bringing up short against a line of rocks. His ears were ringing and he looked up and saw that the sun was blotted out by a thick geysering pall of dust. It was dotted with swirling, tumbling pieces of shattered boulders but what widened his eyes was the sight of the huge, house-sized rock splintering from the blast, spewing out in a torrent of flying granite across the hillside. This swept down the slope away from where he lay and he tried to get to his feet but was kicked prone again by the guard, now dismounted.

'Jesus! The chaingang!' Dakota croaked, knowing the other nine men he had left beneath the trees were in line with the sliding rock and earth. Half the hillside was sweeping down towards them. 'They've used too much dynamite!'

The guard backhanded him, threw him onto his back, unlocked the manacles and the leg irons, dragged him upright.

'You're gonna like this part, Dakota. You

get to hit me,' the guard said with a bitter, crooked smile, and, as Dakota merely stared, he backhanded the prisoner twice, brutally. 'Hit me, you stupid son of a bitch! Hit me, then grab my horse and *go!* Ride south – if you make it *you're free!* I'll say you slugged me in the confusion and stole my mount... *Now do it! Or die where you stand!'*

It sank in immediately and Dakota hit the guard – with a lot more force than the man expected. But this guard had been one of his worst tormentors. Dakota was still holding his manacles and he swung them savagely against the guard's head. The man dropped like a poled steer, spreading out with blood pouring from a deep gash in the side of his head.

Breathing hard, Dakota dropped to one knee, took the man's gun and cartridge belt and swung aboard the horse. *Likely his being armed wasn't supposed to be part of the deal,* he thought. *Too bad! If anyone tried to stop him, he would blow them out of the saddle!*

He had nothing to lose now.

Even as he went over the crest, stretched out along the animal's back, he wondered just what the hell he was getting into.

He meant, well, Judas! What kind of mean son of a bitch would kill a whole work-gang, just to break one man out? Didn't make sense.

And he didn't even know who was behind it.

He rode south, keeping to the timber and brush, and was met and taken into outlaw country, blindfolded for three days while they rode God knew where, and eventually came face to face with the man who had organized his escape.

'Name's Lang Bantry. You've likely heard of me.'

He thrust out his right hand and Dakota gripped with him, looking at the smiling, well-fed face with the neatly trimmed moustache and silver-streaked hair. He was handsome enough but his eyes were way meaner than any Dakota had ever seen. Except on a striking diamondback.

'No, I've never heard of you,' he said and Bantry's smile faltered. He flicked his hard gaze to some of the gun-hung men standing around, then laughed.

'We got us an honest man here, gents! One who ain't afraid to speak up. Well, I like that. Think we're gonna get along pretty good, Dakota.' Bantry squinted suddenly. 'You got another name?'

'Dakota's fine.'

Bantry grinned and shook his head. 'OK, have it your way. Boys, meet "Dakota". He'll be with us for a spell.'

'Doing what?' Dakota asked.

Bantry was sober as he said, 'Why, paying me back for getting you out of Stone Dog. What else?'

Dakota looked around at the hardcases. 'You want me to ride with this bunch?'

'That OK with you?'

Dakota shrugged. 'Not OK, but I'll do what you say – I owe you plenty and I like to square my debts.'

'Oh, don't worry, boy, you'll square away all right. Have to see if you measure up first, though.'

A man named Dewey Haines found a reason to prod Dakota into a fist-fight that very first night in the big camp in the sierras. Haines was big, powerful, looked mean, and wasted no time in knocking Dakota down. Dakota rubbed his throbbing jaw, the men yelling for him to get up, and he thrust up to his feet quickly. On the way he snatched one of the heavy skillets from beside the camp-fire and it made a dull bonging sound as he bounced it off Haines's skull. The ranny staggered, legs turning to jelly. Dakota hit him in the midriff and, when he doubled over, belted him on the back of the head with the skillet, stretching him out.

'I ain't busting my hands on a fool like you.'

As Haines dropped, Dakota faced the others, the heavy pan held out from his side. No one said anything, just turned away and returned to whatever they had been doing before Haines had started things. *It had been a test.*

They gave him a horse with a busted cinchstrap and roared with laughter as he sprawled in the dust, the saddle in his lap. He said nothing, repaired the strap, and rode that frisky horse to a standstill. Next morning, when the rest of the group went to mount, they found all their cinchstraps had been cut.

Dakota didn't bother laughing as the whole gang fell one after the other. One man, calling himself 'Cat', was riled enough to slap a hand against his gun butt. Dakota's right hand blurred and Cat howled as a bullet burned across his knuckles.

They stared: none of them had seen such gun speed.

Watching from the sidelines as usual, Lang

Bantry smiled, nodding quietly to himself.

Three days later, he returned to the camp after a short unexplained absence and asked Dakota:

'Ever been to Stillwater, Texas?'

'Passed through once.'

'Well, it's not all that big. I can draw you a sketch of what I want. You do this for me and we're all squared-away. Ever seen one of these before?'

He unwrapped the long rawhide package he had been holding and handed Dakota the shining Creedmore rifle.

'A beauty, is she not? That's the gun that's going to change the future of the sovereign state of Texas, boy! You got yourself one helluva responsibility, Dakota.' His voice hardened as he added, 'Don't foul up.'

CHAPTER 5

'GET THAT S.O.B!'

'You must've been a damn fool to believe Bantry only wanted the judge wounded!' the girl said with contempt.

He shrugged, worrying about still being in her barn, sure the sheriff would be on his way out here by now with a posse.

'It was no skin off my nose,' Dakota told her. 'I had no love for McManus. I figured I'd shatter his arm, put him through a little hell after the way he sent me to Stone Dog.'

'In other words, you *wanted* to do it?'

'I owed McManus plenty.'

'Couldn't that be why Bantry broke you out of prison?'

He stiffened. 'You mean... set up Mc-Manus to be killed, by one of his own men, but put the blame on me?'

'Yes. Couldn't he have had something to leave behind that would point the finger at you? And because you'd be on the run, no

63

one would doubt you had committed the murder.'

She was surprised when he grinned crookedly.

'I'm not quite as dumb as you think. I figured out something along those lines, but the plan was for me to be found dead, with the Creedmore sniper's rifle in that freighters' warehouse. I would be identified as a man who had threatened to kill the judge, had escaped prison and come to square things...'

She gasped. 'How...?'

'I wanted to take a six-gun with me to that room but Bantry wouldn't hear of it. I could only have the Creedmore rifle – and it was a single shot. Which meant after I'd fired at McManus, the gun would be empty and I would be unarmed. The plan was for someone to come bursting in, shooting, kill me, then say they had heard the gunshot and found me crouched by the window with a smoking rifle. Of course, when my corpse was found, I'd have a six-gun in my hand. Whoever killed me would be the hero...'

She looked at him soberly. 'Obviously their plan didn't work.'

'No. I insisted on seeing the place where they wanted me to shoot from, worked it so that I was in the room by myself for a few minutes by having the feller with me go downstairs and outside to see if he could spot the rifle barrel at the window. In those few minutes, I hid a six-gun – behind a loose wall-board.'

'So you were armed when they came in and tried to kill you?'

He nodded. 'They were amateurs. They were both dead before they'd taken three steps into the room.'

'My God! You are a killer, anyway, aren't you?'

'It was self-defence. Bantry was supposed to have a skiff waiting to take me out of town down the river. There was no escape plan, of course, I had to improvise. And I'm still sorry I had to use your brother. I get the impression you didn't have much time for McManus, anyway.'

'That's my business! Right now, I'm trying to decide what to do about you.'

'Let me take a horse and I'll lead any posse right away from here, say I stole the mount before you woke up.'

She smiled faintly. 'That sounds as if you're expecting to be caught.'

'Well, I don't know this neck of the woods any too well and Bantry'll have it fixed that

I'm to be shot on sight, might even put a bounty out on me. They're holding all the cards now and it's a stacked deck far as I'm concerned.'

She said nothing and, while she was thinking things over, allowed the pitchfork to waver. In an instant he had it in his hands and she staggered, eyes widening as she straightened and saw he had neatly turned the tables. But he didn't menace her with the pitchfork. She backed up against the wall, mighty leery.

'Looks like I get that mount, eh? How about you rope me one from your remuda and I'll be on my way.'

'I – don't think so.'

'Well, we'll see, but I can't waste too much time on you, Miss Darcy.'

'I suppose one more killing won't make any difference to you!'

He arched his eyebrows.

'And here I was thinking you half-way believed me. Not that I can figure why you would...'

Dianna looked a little embarrassed.

'Maybe I believe some of it, but by your own admission you seem to have been a gunfighter and an outlaw before Judge McManus sent you to Stone Dog.'

'I ... was aiming to put all that behind me. That's why I was working that quarter-section, trying to prove up. But seems some of my neighbours were friends of the judge and wanted part of my land and – well, one way and another they got it once McManus put me out of the way.'

'Yes. That influenced me in believing you, in part at least. My family had twice as much land as I have now. There was a dispute and it went before Judge McManus and his decision went against us. We lost more than half our land to Lang Bantry.'

Dakota stiffened. 'Which makes you wonder why he wanted McManus dead. Something to do with him running for governor, I guess...'

He broke off when he saw her face. She was looking beyond his shoulder, out through the barn door, and he spun quickly, tossing aside the fork, drawing his six-gun instinctively. He turned as she gasped and he saw her wide eyes staring at him as she half-covered her mouth with one hand.

'You – I didn't even see that pistol leave the holster!'

But he wasn't interested: he had seen what she had seen.

A swirling dust cloud at this end of the

pass through the hills, way out, but obviously headed this way.

'Now I *have* to get a horse!'

He started towards the door but she grabbed his arm and he came swinging back, the gun rising as if he would strike her. She flinched away, going pale.

'It's too late! You can't ride out without being seen.'

'That's my hard luck.' He drew free of her grip but she came after him, grabbing his arm again with both hands this time. 'Listen, miss, don't you be loco enough to try to stop me or I'll gunwhip you!'

'You are a nasty piece of work, aren't you?' Her eyes narrowed but she seemed to steady herself and said, 'You don't have to go anywhere. You can hide and I'll tell them this is how I found the coffin when I came out of the house and that one of my horses is missing. It's the only way, Dakota! You try to run now and they'll have you by noon!'

He frowned down at her as she released his arm and stepped back. Slowly, he holstered his Colt and nodded curtly.

'If you give me away, you'll be the first to die. You got my word on that.'

Dianna was just driving the last of the

remuda back into the corral when the posse rode into the yard. She was dust-spattered and looked flushed and anxious as Sheriff Doolin reined up; his grim-faced men came to a halt behind him. There were plenty of guns in evidence.

'Hosses get out?' the sheriff asked curtly.

'More like *let* out!' she snapped. 'Linus, will you just take a look in my barn? Go on – go and see what I awoke to this morning!'

Puzzled, the lawman stared at her a long moment. Then he dismounted, took his rifle from the saddle scabbard and gestured to two of the posse men to accompany him to the barn.

They were gone only a minute or so and then Doolin came striding back, face tight, as he shouted:

'Where is he?'

'Is that all you have to say?' Dianna snapped back, choking back a sob, wringing her hands. 'I find my brother's coffin with the lid splintered and empty and all you can say is "Where is he?"'

'Look, I'm sorry, Dianna, but that damn killer gave us the slip in town by ridin' out in Chuck's coffin. Now Chuck's OK. I mean, we found him in another coffin, no harm done, and Overholser is bringin' him out to you and ought to be here right soon. But the feller who killed the judge must've been here. And we're after him! Now – "where is he?"'

'I found my horses running all over the countryside and Chuck's body not where I expected it to be. How would I know where this killer is?'

'His name's Dakota. He escaped from Stone Dog only a few weeks back and he's a cold-blooded murderer. Don't you have nothin' to with him, Dianna. Don't believe nothin' he tells you–'

'My God! D'you think I'm hiding him?'

'No, 'course not, only–'

'You're a tactless man, Linus Doolin! I've always thought so and you've just confirmed it for me.' Angry, she swept an arm around towards the house and barn and the other buildings and lean-tos. 'Search the place if you want– Top to bottom! Go on – I don't mind. I'd rather you did search so you can put your mind at rest and not be suspecting me all the time.'

'God's sake, Dianna! I din' mean to insult you. It's just that we're in a mighty hurry and we don't want that killer to get away.' He detailed three men to start searching, turned back to the girl. 'Any of your hosses missing?'

She hesitated, then nodded.

'A claybank. One of my saddles, too. He must've kicked his way out of the coffin, taken the horse and saddle, then driven the others out to cover his tracks...'

Doolin smothered a curse.

'You never heard nothin'?'

She shook her head.

'I – took a couple of glasses of brandy to make me sleep.'

'Yeah, sure – understandable...' Doolin was impatient, bawling to the men who were in the house and other buildings. 'Hurry it up! We've got to get this S.O.B!'

But no one had found any sign of Dakota.

'He would've headed for the hills, I suppose,' Dianna said. 'Does he know the country?'

'Dunno. We don't know that much about him, but I suspect you're right. He'd make for the hills. Well, we'll water our hosses and get goin'. Don't see no reason why he might come back but you keep a shotgun handy just in case, hear?' She nodded as he mounted and added, 'Overholser ought to be along pretty soon. Sure sorry you had to go through this, Dianna.'

She said nothing, watched them water their mounts, then ride out, making for the distant hills. Back in the other direction, she saw a small dust cloud at the pass and her stomach tightened as she realized this was probably the undertaker bringing Chuck's body to her...

Overholser had company.

Sitting beside him on the buckboard seat, his mount tied to the tailgate, was Deputy Marvin Torres, his hat sitting all askew because of the bandage wrapped around his head.

He climbed down a little shakily when the undertaker hauled rein in the ranch yard, lifted a hand to his hatbrim. He looked a little grey under his naturally swarthy skin.

'Howdy, Dianna. Figured I could lend a hand to bury Chuck. Big job for a lady on her own.'

'That's good of you, Marv, but...' She gestured to his head and he touched the bandage lightly, his narrow face tightening.

'Yeah. This Dakota *hombre* laid me out with my own shotgun. Humiliatin'. The saw-bones'll be climbin' the walls when he finds out I quit his blamed infirmary but Doolin was too impatient to wait. I want my chance at this sonuver – pardon – this... killer.' He shook his head slowly. 'I can't stand bein' made to look a fool.'

'Well, you shouldn't overdo things, Marv. Head injuries are always chancy...'

Overholser was puffing at the tailgate, lowering it and uncovering the coffin containing the mortal remains of Chuck Darcy.

'You wanna lend a hand here, Marv? If you're feelin' as spry as you figure you are.'

'Spry or not you ain't gonna be able to lift that down yourself,' growled the deputy, going to the rear of the buckboard.

'I'd've just had to rig a couple boards to slide it off, wouldn't I,' grouched the undertaker.

'We can all manage it,' the girl said tightly, feeling her nerves twanging now. 'I – haven't even got the grave dug, I'm afraid.'

'We'll do that for you,' Torres said, glaring at Overholser who looked appalled at the thought of real manual labour.

There was a deal of bickering and quiet cussing on the men's part but between the three of them they had Chuck laid to rest in a couple of hours.

It had taken a lot out of Torres, and Overholser sat spread-legged under a tree clasping his chest as sweat drenched him, murmuring something about an imminent heart attack.

But they all survived and Dianna supplied coffee laced with whiskey and day-old biscuits reheated and that seemed to pick them up. Just before noon, Overholser turned his buckboard and drove back towards the pass and town. Dianna looked a question at Torres who was checking the saddle on his tough little grulla mount.

'Are you going to try to catch up with the posse, Marv?'

'Guess so.'

'They made for the hills.'

'Yeah, that'd be the place to look. Any tracks?'

She shook her head. 'He let loose my remuda and ran it over the yard to hide them.'

Torres looked at her sharply. 'Smart *hombre*. Which makes you wonder if he would make for the hills as anyone would expect...?'

The girl frowned. 'Where else could he go – and hope to hide? They say he doesn't know the country.'

'Yeah – s'pect you're right.'

Torres mounted stiffly, waved and, with Dianna's thanks ringing in his ears, rode out of the yard in the same direction taken by the posse.

The girl watched from the porch until he was lost in the shadows of the first foothills and then turned back into the small ranch house.

Inside, she watched through the curtains of the parlour windows, waiting to see Torres come out on the trail that climbed up into the mountains. She glimpsed him but he wasn't as far up as she expected and she frowned, her teeth tugging at her lower lip.

She went to the kitchen, picked up a woven Indian basket she used for carrying vegetables from the root cellar and crossed the yard to the cellar's entrance. She looked around casually as she threw back the plank door, then climbed down the steep stairs into the dim coolness of the earth. Shelves were lined with jars of preserves and vegetables and other perishables were stacked in a corner.

She jumped a little when something moved in the opposite corner and Dakota stepped out, lowering the hammer on the pistol he held as he holstered it.

'I – I thought you'd still be in the safe box.'

'Lady, I've had enough of coffins and coffin-like spaces. I was down in the ground there for more then two hours waiting for the goddamn posse to go. I didn't aim to

75

drown in my own sweat any longer.'

'Well, I guess I can understand.' She cast a glance towards the area of floor just under the wall shelves. On the bottom, if the jars of pickles were moved, two floorboards lifted and exposed an opening into a dark cavity large enough for a couple of adults or three children or, at a squeeze, two kids and an adult. Her father had built this refuge when she and Chuck were kids and the Comanche had been raising hell with the settlers in the region. It had served them well and she had immediately thought of it when she had decided to hide out Dakota from the posse.

Actually, she was still puzzled as to why she more than half-way believed this man's story. She knew she leaned towards it partly because she had hated – no, that wasn't too strong a word – Judge McManus for his corruption and his having aided Lang Bantry to steal their land. But there was also a sincerity in Dakota she hadn't expected and certainly hadn't been looking for. It had surprised her when she realized just how much of his story she was willing to accept as gospel.

Anyway, she was involved now whether she liked it or not – and whether he had told her the truth or only part of it.

'I'm obliged for all you've done, Dianna,' Dakota told her. 'I've eaten some of your preserves, some radish and green beans. Mighty fine peaches and pears. Didn't know they grew so well down here.'

'They're a lot of work, have to be nurtured well. My mother was the one with the green thumb. I seem to have inherited some of it. Doolin's posse are searching the hills and that deputy you knocked out after the shooting – Torres – is keen to catch up with you. His head is still bandaged but he quit the infirmary and rode after the posse when he'd finished here...'

He was watching her closely as she spoke and when she paused he waited and asked, 'Something else?'

'I'm not sure. I watched to see if he did actually ride up into the hills and he did. But I don't think he took the trail up the mountain. He seemed to veer off, but I couldn't be certain because of the timber.'

'Which way d'you think he went?'

She hesitated. 'If he went the way I think – it would be west.'

Dakota tightened his lips.

'Damn! That's the way I was going to go – ride below the skyline and cut down to Cougar Creek.'

She looked at him sharply. 'I thought you didn't know this country?'

'Don't. But Bantry drew me a map, put in alternative escape routes – just to make me feel the whole deal was on the up-and-up, I guess.'

'Well, you can make Cougar Creek that way, but there's a stage swing-station right above it on the smallest range. You'd have to keep well clear or you'd be seen.'

'Thanks. Now, how about that horse? I can't pay you right now. I've only got a few dollars, but I'll send you whatever you think it's worth soon as I get clear.'

She smiled. 'You sound confident!'

He shrugged. 'Know what's happening now. I was set up and I was looking at things from a different angle when I thought all I was doing was a favour to Lang Bantry. Now I know I'm running for my life and that's the way I'll go about it...'

She filled the basket quickly with some vegetables and placed a jar of preserved apples on top, then climbed up into the sunlight of the yard again.

She stood there by the door, seeming to look around as if enjoying the day, perhaps trying to come to terms with the fact that she had so recently buried her only brother, for the benefit of anyone watching. Then she said quietly as she rearranged the jar on the vegetables in the basket, without turning around,

'It's all clear. I'll pack you a grub sack. Take that big grey with the black circle round its eye. It's a gelding and strong. More strong than fast but muscle is what you need if you're going to be riding to Cougar Creek.'

As she heard Dakota start up the steps, she failed to see the brief flash up amongst the timber of the foothills where Marvin Torres had ridden.

It might have been sun glinting off the lenses of a pair of field glasses.

CHAPTER 6

HUNT THE MAN DOWN

Dakota was stiff from his long sojourn in cramped spaces and his hips seemed to creak as he set the big grey with the black-circled eye out of the ranch yard. He didn't turn west right away, but rode towards a place about midway between the pass and the trail to the hills.

He kept his head down but he was looking around and up as he rode. *There!* Just a brief glint as something moved in the shadow of some rocks. He thought he had caught a similar flash out of the corner of his eye while he was saddling the grey. Someone was watching from up there.

Well, that was okay up to a point. At least he knew now he was being observed. Hardest thing to do would be to ride and make his movements look as if he was totally unaware of the watcher. Might be that deputy... He seemed to have a hate on for Dakota because he had been slugged with his own shotgun. Man who would leave his sickbed to come after a fugitive like that must have a mighty powerful bitterness driving him.

Of course, a man like Doolin probably rubbed it in roughly, showing little sympathy for Torres's injuries. *That* could drive a man just as powerfully as hate. Not that it mattered. *Someone, for whatever reason*, was up there watching him and Dakota knew he would need to be mighty vigilant himself from here on in.

He had to ride towards the point he had originally been making for, because the trail that eventually led to Cougar Creek had its beginnings up there in that broken country. He had consulted the crude sketch-map that Bantry had given him before the shooting of McManus.

'In case you have to improvise, Dakota,' Lang Bantry had told him with a friendly grin, 'if for some reason we can't get you away down river you might have to make a run for the hills. Oh, we'll have a man to take you out of here safely, but if things should go wrong and you're on your own, this sketch'll help get you clear.'

Dakota hoped the man was right.

He found a couple of landmarks, but a

third one he needed in order to locate the edge of the old trail didn't seem to be where it ought to be. It was a broken topped pine. He wondered how long since Bantry had been up this way? Could the pine have grown a new top since the man had last seen it? Or had the pine even existed?

There was this hunch gnawing away at him, a hunch that the map might be worthless and following it would only lead him into trouble. The girl had given him some verbal directions and he decided to follow them and see where they led.

He was still puzzled as to why she was helping him after first making it clear that not only did she doubt his story but she showed signs of actually hating the type of man she had decided he was. Well, to hell with it, anyway. Main thing was she *was* helping him: she had given him a mount and a grub sack and even a carbine with ammunition, saying it had belonged to Chuck.

It had prompted him to ask where were the rest of her ranch hands and she had surprised him by saying that she and Chuck had been trying to run the place between them. Bantry's men had beaten up some of the hands she had hired and he had bought up some of the stores in town. Her credit was fast running out. She couldn't afford to hire hands and, in fact, one reason she took on the chore of burying Chuck herself was because of a lack of funds.

He felt that someone who was open enough to tell him those things was to be trusted – as far as he could bring himself to trust anyone. Long ago he had decided that no one, but *no one*, was to be trusted, and that was especially true when a man had spent as long a time behind bars as Dakota had.

Thirty-two years old and a third of that time had been spent in prisons and local law's cell blocks. That was what had made him decide to try and make a fist of straight living when he had set out to prove up on that quarter-section.

He was riding through a dry wash now. It was taking a snake-turn downslope and towards the west, which seemed to lead in the direction he wanted to go. He paused long enough to take out Bantry's sketch but didn't actually study it: he used it as a cover while he looked around. No sign of anyone following but he would bet that deputy or whoever it had been with the field glasses was back there somewhere, focusing on him right this minute.

He was right and he was wrong.

Right in that it was Deputy Torres, wrong in that he was focusing his field glasses on Dakota.

What the lawman was doing was drawing a bead on the fugitive, sighting carefully along the flat top of his rifle barrel, elbow supported on his crushed hat on top of a rock. He had figured out which way Dakota was headed, knew he had to come through this dry wash, and had ridden on ahead, screened by timber and low ridges.

He was actually slightly ahead and a little above Dakota.

But he shouldn't have taken off his hat: his white bandages caught the brilliant sunlight and made a bright spot to draw Dakota's eye. The fugitive saw the white flare of the bandages and reacted instinctively, throwing himself sideways out of the saddle, on the upslope side so he didn't have so far to fall, and snatched the carbine free of the short scabbard as he went.

Torres's lead punched through the air space left by Dakota's tumbling body and whined away from a rock behind. The grey snorted and stamped to find firm footing and by then Dakota was sliding down slope, carbine held out to one side for balance, pushing against the ground with his free hand, guiding his body in behind some rocks. Two more bullets kicked dust from those rocks as he scrabbled in behind, rolling off his back and levering a shell into the carbine's breech as he did so. He sent three rapid shots up at the rock where he had spotted the bandages and saw the blur of white as Torres hurriedly ducked. Dakota levered again, lunged to the side so that he landed behind bigger rocks and then crouched on one knee, replacing the three used shells – just in case Torres was counting.

There were two more shots from up above but they were wild and Dakota smiled thinly: Torres had lost him.

Good! He moved right along the line of big rocks as they grew into full-fledged boulders. He clambered between them, heard two fast shots and rapidly whining ricochets, the sound telling him that Torres was shooting in desperation now: he was bouncing his bullets off narrow spaces, ricocheting them from rockface to rockface, hoping they would find Dakota crouching there.

Dakota held his fire, working out by the crash of the rifle where Torres had to be.

The man had moved a little higher and more to his left. Dakota went up between the large boulders, squeezing through in a couple of places, having to remove his hat and turn his head awkwardly to make it. But he got where he wanted to go, stretched out on the top of an elongated boulder, crawling across, belly to sandstone. He flipped himself off just before the end – and just before Torres saw him and opened up in a wild volley.

Rockdust and spattering lead stung Dakota's upper arms and shoulders as he slid off the rock head first, desperately somersaulting just before he hit the ground. It knocked the wind out of him but he tried to keep moving even though it hurt like hell as he fought to drag air down into his lungs. He jumped forward awkwardly and Torres stood up on his rock, rifle to shoulder, shooting down in a series of raking shots.

Dakota spun onto his back, carbine across his chest, levered and triggered in a fast, deafening volley. Torres started to duck and the first bullet hit and flung him off his rock as if he had been jerked by a wire. In mid-air the second slug arched his body: he twisted head down and fell out of sight.

Dakota heard the man's rifle clatter as it

fell from his hands.

He was sure Torres was out of action now, but he took the time to reload the rifle and to check his Colt, easing it in the holster for a fast draw if necessary.

Crouching, he made his way out of the boulder-field going upslope until he was high enough to look down beyond the huge boulders that had hidden the ambusher.

Torres lay unmoving, just beyond the shadows cast by the granite. Dakota covered him, walked warily across to the edge of the rock where he was standing and stepped onto the one directly above the deputy. Torres moaned and Dakota saw the blood then, smeared across the boulder, and some splashed on the ground. The deputy grunted and slowly turned over onto his left side. His right hand groped down into a wound on that side and there was blood showing on his hip lower down. The man's eyes turned up and saw Dakota standing there, covering him with the carbine.

'You're – pretty damn – good – killer!' gasped the deputy.

Dakota said nothing, watching.

'You gonna – finish – it?'

'You'll live – if you don't bleed to death.'

'Damn you! – I – I...'

The effort was too much for him and he slumped, his hand falling away from his side, revealing the ragged hole in the shirt – and the bloody wound in the flesh. Dakota could see the whiteness of bone showing, likely a rib. Must be mighty painful, he reckoned.

Torres lay there, eyes glazing but full of black hatred for the man who had shot him.

'I'll leave you your six-gun,' Dakota said abruptly, and turned, leaping from rock to rock until he made it down into the wash where the grey waited patiently, having located a patch of grass to browse on.

He thought Torres called something after him but couldn't be sure. He wondered if the sound of gunfire had reached the posse across in the hills but he doubted it: they had had too long a lead to be within earshot. Well, Torres would likely find his way back to the Darcy place and no doubt Dianna would tend his wounds – if he made it.

One thing was for sure: Dakota didn't aim to hang around this neck of the woods.

Sheriff Linus Doolin lifted a hand and then pushed his hat back from his face, mopped his forehead with his shirt sleeve. He hooked a boot around the saddle horn with a grunt, took out cigarette papers and tobacco sack, and built a smoke slowly as the posse behind came to a ragged halt.

They were high in the hills and looked out over the afternoon mist starting to form in the hollows below. There was still timber above them but it was petering out and the bare peaks rose against the sky.

'If that son of a bitch came up this high, he must be plumb loco,' he growled and a gangling man with wide mouth and watery eyes beside him grunted.

'Dunno what we're doin' way up here, Linus.'

Doolin snapped his head around sharply.

'I mean,' the man added, 'we ain't even found any tracks, just tried to outguess him – and I'd say we ain't doin' too good.'

'Say what you like,' Doolin snapped, lighting his cigarette. 'We done our best with what we had to go on. I'm just wonderin' if that Darcy woman told us the truth.'

Several of the posse within earshot looked quickly at the lawman.

'Hell, sheriff, why wouldn't she?'

'Yeah, Linus. That killer dumped her brother outta his *coffin*, for Chrissakes!'

'Dianna Darcy is a fine woman.'

Doolin raked his hard gaze around the weary, sweaty riders. 'I know that.'

'Town's behind her, too,' went on the man who claimed she was a fine woman. 'I mean, it's time you did somethin' about that Roy Callahan, an' young Chuck Darcy was OK. He never bothered folk much, just started thinkin' below his belt when he met that whore–'

'We ain't here to be talkin' about a dead man!' Doolin snapped. 'We're here to hunt down Dakota – and we ain't havin' much luck. So I say we go back to town and get properly organized and make a fresh start tomorrow. We'll split up, some takin' the other part of the hills, others workin' the low country, movin' towards Cougar Creek.'

'Hell, if he went that way he's long gone!'

'We *look*, damnit! We search and hunt and live rough until we find him.'

Doolin was in no mood to be argued with. The posse men knew it so they turned back down the long, shadowing slopes with a sigh. At least they could sleep in their own beds tonight.

After that, who knew where they'd end up?

It was well after dark when the posse rode back into town and told the folk who rushed

91

to greet them that they had had no luck. They went to their own homes and Doolin, carrying his rifle and war bag, made for his office.

Two men were waiting for him, a lamp burning low on his desk. Lang Bantry sat at his ease in Doolin's chair while a big man perched one gun-hung hip on a corner of the desk, smoking. As Doolin paused in the doorway, this man ground out his cigarette on the desk top, stood and walked across to the sheriff. It was a kind of mincing walk but Doolin knew it was the kind of shuffle that a bear used, well-balanced, flatfooted and solid. It would take a straining horse to push such a man off his feet.

'Mr Bantry's been waitin', Doolin.'

'Use an ashtray next time, Roy,' the sheriff snapped at the big man. He stepped around him and dumped his war bag, stood his rifle butt-down in the rack and hung up his hat. Bantry drew on his cigar, watching him through the smoke.

'Been wasting your time in the hills, I hear, Linus.'

'Not wastin' time, Lang. Doin' our best with what we had to work with. Which wasn't much.'

'Tell me.'

Doolin told him.

'You believed that girl?'

'Don't see why she'd lie. I mean, that killer dumped her brother outta his own coffin and–'

'She's a troublemaker, has been for years. All the Darcys were trouble-makers, even that kid brother of hers.' Bantry flicked his eyes briefly to the big man. 'Roy settled that part, though.'

Doolin stiffened. 'You mean – you *fixed* it so Chuck'd be loco enough to challenge Roy to a gunfight?'

'Never mind that. I want Dakota hunted down and *killed!* I was a good friend of Judge McManus and Dakota double-crossed me and killed him. I want that son of a bitch shot on sight! This town, all of Texas, has to see I don't stand by and see my friends murdered and do nothing about it. Now you pass the word along to your damn posse, whenever you get around to go looking for Dakota again. And tell them, the man who nails Dakota gets a thousand bucks from me. OK?'

Doolin flushed, not a man to be told by anyone, but he wasn't about to cross swords with Bantry. He nodded jerkily.

'I'll get it done, Lang. We'll go properly

93

prepared for a long stay this time. And your reputation'll be OK.'

Bantry stood abruptly, startling the sheriff, making him step back hurriedly.

'Not *too* damn long a time! I want Dakota dead, *pronto!* I'm sending Roy along to help.'

Doolin raised his eyes slowly to the tight-lipped, squint-eyed Callahan.

'That ain't necessary, Lang.'

'I said Roy'll be riding with you.'

'Hell, I can do this! I know my job, damnit! And I don't need no gunslinger ridin' herd on me!'

Bantry looked at Callahan. The big man stepped forward swiftly and drove a fist into the sheriff's kidneys. Doolin staggered face first into the wall. Callahan spread a hand on the back of his head and rammed him into the woodwork above the gun rack again. Doolin's legs buckled a little. Callahan spun him around, grabbed his shirt front and drew back his right fist.

Bantry signed to him to hold up.

'I think Linus understands now. Right, Sheriff?'

Bleeding from the nose and a scrape above his right eye, Doolin fumbled off his necker-chief and nodded. There was no fear showing in his eyes but his whole manner had changed.

'Yeah, Lang. Whatever you say.'

'That's the way it always is – and better be. I expect you to have cleared town with a bigger posse before sun-up, Linus. You get some rest now.'

Callahan opened the street door and held it for Bantry and then followed him out into the night.

Doolin slumped in his chair, holding his neckerchief against his oozing nostrils.

'Damn it to hell!' he said aloud, the words coming back at him off the four walls of the small office.

They didn't make him feel any better.

But Bantry was the one footing the bill so he had to accept it ... or pay the consequences.

CHAPTER 7

TURNAROUND

Torres was in terrible pain. He had been unable to stop the bleeding from his side although he had wadded a kerchief over the wound and had even managed to tear the tail off his shirt and hold that in place.

But it still oozed blood and every breath he took was like a dozen knives driving into his lungs. The other wound wasn't bothering him much but he was feeling very light-headed and thirsty. He had tried to crawl out of the rocks to where he had hidden his horse but had made no more than a few feet before he had to give up. He sprawled, exhausted, tongue swelling, wild thoughts swirling around inside his head. One moment his skin felt as if it was burning up, rough and ready to split, the next he was shivering.

Sometime after sundown he passed out and groaned and tossed fitfully with the frightening dreams that filled his fevered brain...

He didn't know what time it was when he awoke.

At first he thought it was part of the nightmares but then he felt the hand on his arm and his eyes flew wide. He could just make out the shape of a man kneeling beside him.

'Wh–who...?'

'Dakota. Just lie still. I'm gonna flush that wound with some water and it'll sting like hell. Then I'll bind it up to give you some support, so prepare for a lot of pain.'

'You! Judas, first – you shoot a – man – ride off – then come back – an'–'

Torres bit back a scream as the cold water flooded into the wound. Working only by feel, Dakota flushed out some of the gravel and shredded cloth that had been forced in by the bullet and the deputy's writhings. If Marv Torres thought that was painful, he was in for a shock when the fugitive started to wrap some cloth around the wound with a clean pad covering it. He punched weakly, cursing a blue streak, but the words blurred and he slumped back and eventually passed out.

When he came to, he was roped in his saddle and Dakota was leading his horse up a steep trail. Torres moaned and Dakota hipped in the saddle of the grey.

'You with us?'

'Ye-ah. Why – why're you – doin' this?'

Dakota was silent a moment and then said:

'Trade you. I take you to the stage swing-station and leave you outside and you tell me how to find the trail to Cougar Creek.'

It took a while for the words to sink in and then, despite his pain and splitting head, Torres grinned.

'Got yourself lost, huh?'

'I was given a map. It's all wrong. It was leading me back and around to the foothills of the main range. Where the posse is likely looking for me.'

'Yeah, that's where Doolin was goin'. Who gave you the map? Man who paid you to kill the judge?'

'I didn't kill McManus. We got a deal?'

Torres was quiet again for a time.

'What if I say no?'

'I'll leave you near the swing station and try to find the way to Cougar Creek myself.'

The deputy even managed a brief laugh.

'How you gonna do that in the dark?'

'Use the stars. I've got a rough notion where the creek is.'

'You din' have to come back then, did you...?' Torres stopped as his own words sank in. 'No! You din' *have* to come back at all! You could've used the stars anyways – and you've told me where you're headed now. You come back to help *me!*'

'Now why would I do that?' Dakota said in clipped tones.

'Mebbe you ain't such a cold-blooded murderer as they say. Just – mebbe ...'

'Told you, I didn't kill McManus. You can tell Doolin that when you see him, but don't worry about it, *amigo*. Am I headed in the right direction for the swing station?'

Torres had to concentrate hard but he looked around him, not making out much in the faint light thrown out by a sliver of a moon in the east. But he knew his stars, too, and he said:

'More to the east, but we can't move off this slope until we reach the top. Then branch right and you'll find the stage road over the crest...'

He fell silent and likely passed out two or three times before they stopped again. The lack of motion brought him back to consciousness. They were on the crest of a rise and he saw the pale width of the narrow stage road angling down into the hollow where the lights of the swing station showed.

It was a cluster of only three buildings, the

largest being the stage office and an area where weary travellers could have a drink of coffee and perhaps a snack. The others were the stables and corrals and a lean-to where any mechanical troubles on a stagecoach could be attended to. Only a dim light showed in the rear of the main building.

'We – here?' Torres asked, words slurred with pain.

'Can you ride on down yourself?'

'Try...'

But when Dakota turned loose the reins, the first few steps taken by Torres's horse flung the wounded man to one side so that he was leaning against the ropes, groaning with the pain the position caused him.

Dakota reached for the reins again.

'I'll take you down – I'll leave you outside.'

Torres nodded, tried to mumble his thanks but couldn't get the words out. Then he said:

'I seen you runnin' away. That's when you hit me with my own shotgun. You *had* to've been the killer.'

'No – there was someone else fired the same time as me. I was setup.'

'Likely story!'

'Only one I've got and it's gospel. Now, shut up.' Dakota led the horses down, walking beside his grey, holding the bridle of Torres's mount, the deputy swaying against the restraining ropes. He paused about five yards from the building, put the reins in Torres's hands and mounted the grey.

'Hold on tight in case your bronc spooks when I fire my gun. Now, which is the quickest way to Cougar Creek?'

Torres lifted his heavy head slowly. His voice was raspy.

'Go back to the top of the rise – veer north-west from the road, cut left at the rock pile. It's steep and your hoss might slide. Takes you down into a draw. Creek's a mile past the draw, due west... Listen, feller – I – I'm obliged. I – won't mention Cougar Creek – right away – I'll be delirious or unconscious. But I'll have to mention it – eventually.'

'That's OK I ought to be long gone by then. Hope you make it...'

As he drew his gun and fired the first shot into the night, Torres murmured:

'You, too...'

As the third shot hammered through the night a man burst out of the outhouse along-side the main building, holding his trousers with one hand, a sixgun in the other. He was only yards from Dakota and he fired wildly.

Dakota whirled the grey and spurred for the top of the slope again, bullets whistling around him. The grey stumbled on the broken ground, then he was flying through the timber and skidding over the crest, hearing shouting voices down below at the swing station.

'Hell, I thought it was Injuns!' panted the man who had burst out of the privy, buckling his belt now.

'No – he – he was just leavin' me...' grated Torres. 'He's OK– O ... K.'

He slumped against the ropes and the other two men who had come running out of the main building, guns in hands, turned to the wounded man.

'We better get this feller inside – he's in a bad way,' said a bearded man in filthy buckskins. He glanced up the slope where they could still hear the fading sounds of Dakota's mount. 'That feller sure was in a hurry not to say howdy...'

'Has an urgent message for someone out on the llano,' gasped Torres, lying as well as his fevered mind would let him. 'He's – OK...'

'So you keep sayin',' said one of the men.

'Let's get him inside...'

Deep down in the draw, Dakota discovered that it hadn't only been the broken ground that had made his horse stumble.

One of those wild bullets had taken the animal just forward of the right hip. The wound was bleeding quite badly, the bullet still in there somewhere.

The blood was already splashing all over the slope.

Dianna Darcy opened the house door cautiously, a rifle in her hands.

It was barely daylight and she peered out, frowning, at the bearded man in dirty buckskins standing on her ricketty porch. Behind him she saw a man slumped in the saddle, held there by ropes, his torso bare except for a swathe of grimy-looking bandages, more bandages around his head. A riderless mount stood patiently beside the wounded man's horse.

The buckskinner touched a hand to his shapeless, greasy hat. 'Morg Rance from the swing station, ma'am.'

'I know who you are, Mr Rance. Is that Deputy Marv Torres you have there?'

'Yes'm. Some feller dropped him off at the swing station last night. He's shot-up pretty bad, seems to've lost a lot of blood. There ain't a stage through till sundown today and I figured mebbe he better have some proper attention long before then. Your place was closest. Mebbe you can have one of your men take him into town to a doctor?'

She didn't want to tell him she was here alone, although he likely knew and was simply playing dumb.

'I'll have a look at him and take him into town later, perhaps. Do you need help to get him inside?'

'I can manage, ma'am, and I'm obliged.'

She had Rance put the unconscious deputy in what used to be Chuck's bedroom, brought hot water and clean cloths and then used scissors to cut away the grimy bandages covering Torres's wound.

'These dirty rags won't help,' she said curtly and Morg Rance shuffled his feet.

'We ain't got much to work with up there, ma'am.'

As she cleaned the wound and dabbed iodine around it, causing the deputy to moan and jerk, she asked as casually as she could:

'Who brought him to the way station Mr Rance?'

'That I dunno, ma'am – Torres din' say. He's been out to it most of the time. Hondo, our wrangler, thought we was bein' attacked and started shootin'. He thinks he either winged the feller or his mount. Found some blood on the ground and one of the tree trunks. Can't blame Hondo. We've been losin' the odd hoss outta the corrals. Bucks from the reservation, I guess. We get a bit edgy...'

'I'm sure no one will blame anyone, Mr Rance,' Dianna said a little breathlessly, wondering if Dakota had been wounded. Also wondering how Torres had sustained his wounds and why Dakota had shown some humanity and taken him in to the way station... *It had to've been him!*

'You need me any more, ma'am? We got a lotta work to get done before that stage this evenin'...?'

'No, I'll manage, thank you, Mr Rance. Perhaps you'd like a cup of coffee and some breakfast before you leave? I'll only be a few minutes here. The deputy is unconscious but his breathing is steady enough...'

'Right kind of you, ma'am. I'm obliged.'

When Rance had left, Dianna returned to Chuck's room, stood beside the bed looking down at Torres, who seemed to be sleeping.

'You don't have to pretend to be unconscious any longer, Marv. Rance has gone.'

There was no response at first but, when she pulled a chair up and sat down, obviously prepared to wait, the deputy's eyes flickered open and he gave her a faint smile.'

'Didn't want them questionin' me.'

'Did Dakota do this to you?'

Torres hesitated but nodded, told her about the ambush, how Dakota had ridden out and then come back.

'Said he'd trade: tend my wound and take me to the swing station if I told him how to find Cougar Creek.' He paused. 'Someone had given him a map that was all wrong, was gonna lead him back to where the posse was searchin'.'

She said nothing.

'Queer, ain't it? Almost like someone *wanted* him to ride straight into Doolin.'

'I'm sure I don't know. All that riding roped in a saddle hasn't helped this wound much, Marv. It's torn the edges and I think it needs suturing and probably a much better flushing out than I can give it. I think I'll have to take you into town.'

He nodded, watching her face.

'Dakota was riding that grey with the ring round his eye from your remuda. I thought you said it was a claybank that was missin'.'

'Did I? Possibly I did – I was a little confused and fussed at the time, I guess. D'you think if I support you you could get to the buckboard if I bring it up to the porch?'

'I'll make it. Look, Dianna. I know you helped Dakota. I dunno why, but I know you helped him. I watched you give him that grey from the hills there through field glasses.'

Her teeth tugged at her lower lip and she wouldn't look at him.

'Can't figure out why you'd help a man who messed with Chuck that way. Unless you thought he was gettin' a raw deal in some way...?'

'What kind of raw deal? I don't understand you.'

'Don't get all fussed now. Look, Dakota told me he didn't shoot the judge, that there was another man who fired the same time as he did. He din' go into detail but I found myself ready to believe him. First, I thought it was just 'cause he'd come back to help me, but – I dunno. There was somethin' about him –and him bein' given a fake map that seemed like it was meant to get him into trouble... I'd like to know why you decided to help him. You must've believed whatever story he told you.'

After a time she said quietly: 'He didn't tell me much. I'm afraid that, like you, I simply followed a hunch. Some of his – actions – weren't in keeping with a man who was a cold-blooded murderer. And I think he demonstrated again when he came back to tend you and take you to the stage station that he has a – decency in him. A quite strong decency.'

Torres nodded, hanging on now, feeling the strain of the night overtaking him, wanting to plunge him into a darkness not of his making.

'I – guess that's – it – I dunno. I try to be a good lawman but it's – hard at times with Doolin bein' such a sorehead about everythin'. I know he had ... dealin's with Judge McManus and Lang Bantry that weren't goin' by the book. But what can you do when you're only a deputy?'

'The thing is, Marv, what're you going to do now?'

He frowned, still hanging on tightly so he would be lucid in his answer.

'I – I'll think about it on the way to – town...'

Then he slumped unconscious.

The sun was shining brightly when she saw the posse coming up the trail towards her.

Dianna reined down, almost standing on

the brake bar and the buckboard slewed a little. In the back, Torres made a startled sound.

'It's the posse!' she said over her shoulder. 'Twice as big as before! And – my God, Roy Callahan is with them!'

'That don't sound good,' Torres grated. 'Look, I made my own way down to your place, OK? I'll tell some story about Dakota and me shootin' it out in the foothills.'

'Here comes Doolin and Callahan!' she interrupted and nodded to the men as they reined up.

'Who you got there?' demanded the sheriff and started when he saw it was his deputy. 'Judas priest, Marv! What in hell happened?'

'Was trailin' you into the foothills. Spotted Dakota makin' a run for it towards the pass and we traded lead. He got me but I managed to get back to Dianna's...'

'Towards the *pass?*' echoed Roy Callahan sceptically. 'The hell would he be doin' goin' back through the pass?'

'I didn't say he went through. He was ridin' in that direction was all. Could've turned back into the hills so's he'd miss the posse...'

'Yeah, likely that's what the sonuver did,' allowed Doolin. 'You all right, Marv?'

'He needs to see a doctor.' Dianna answered for him. 'It's a bad wound and he's lost a lot of blood.'

'We're gonna sweep the hills this time,' Doolin told Torres. 'The orders are to shoot on sight.'

'Isn't that a little drastic?' the girl asked breathlessly.

Callahan answered: 'Man kills the next governor of Texas and you want we should bring him in alive, spend money feedin' him and so on and then run a trial at citizens' expense before we hang him anyway...?'

'I was thinking that if you brought him in alive you could at least find out *why* he killed Judge McManus.'

'That's easy, Dianna,' the sheriff said. 'Revenge –'cause the judge put him away in Stone Dog. No, we don't need to *talk* to Dakota. Just kill him before he kills anyone else.'

CHAPTER 8

'GOT HIM!'

'She's lyin',' Callahan said as the posse headed for the hills.

Doolin, riding ahead of the main body of men with the gunslinger, nodded slowly.

'Had that notion, too. But we gotta handle her carefully. Town's right behind her because of Chuck, you know. They figure she's had a rough time of it.'

Callahan gave a crooked smile as he swung his head towards the sheriff.

'That right? Well, the hell with the town and her, too. Bantry wants that son of a bitch *nailed*, but good, and we do whatever it takes. You notice she had *two* mounts tied to the tailgate of that buckboard? One was Torres's but the other, that buckskin, he's from her remuda. Used to see Chuck ridin' it.'

Doolin frowned. 'Likely gonna sell it to the livery. Caleb Fields made Chuck an offer and after Chuck was killed I heard him tell Dianna he'd give her a good price if she was short of cash. Which he knows damn well she is.'

Roy Callahan wasn't a man who was willing to see every side of every story. He had his own notions and his own hunches to follow. He reined aside, catching the sheriff unawares, and as the lawman pulled over to him the gunslinger took out tobacco sack and papers, waving the straggling posse men on as he started to build a cigarette.

'S'pose you and the others scout the hills like you planned, Linus. I dunno why, but I think Torres was lyin' about where he shot it out with Dakota.'

'What're you gettin' at?'

'Like I said, you go on into the hills with the posse. Me, I'm goin' back to town.'

Doolin started. 'The hell for?'

'See what the Darcy woman's up to. She'll take Torres to the sawbones – but I doubt she's gonna sell that buckskin. The saddle-bags looked full lyin' in the buckboard alongside Marv. I'm bettin' it's grub, and there were two big saddle canteens there, too, peekin' out from under a blanket.'

'So...?'

Callahan made an exasperated sound as he lit the cigarette and exhaled smoke.

'She's gonna go find Dakota! Christ,

Linus, how d'you hold down that sheriff's job bein' so dumb?'

'Watch your goddamn mouth! Just because you think you're fastest man with a gun ever lived, don't mean you are!'

Callahan looked briefly surprised then laughed, 'Judas, you *challengin'* me?'

'No. But you don't have to die by someone who's faster, Roy. I mean, look at McManus, how he died. Never knew what hit him...'

Callahan's smiled faded.

'Why, you damn fool! Don't you threaten *me!* Listen, you heard what Bantry said. I'm in charge now, just don't shout it out so the others know. But *you* know, Linus! And you do what you're told.'

Doolin tightened his lips, glared but nodded jerkily. He had no wish to cross Lang Bantry but he wasn't afraid of Callahan despite the man's murderous reputation.

'All right. But s'pose she *is* just sellin' the hoss to Fields?'

'Then I come back and join you. But I reckon before sundown I'll have that son of a bitch Dakota in my sights.'

'Have 'em centred on his back, I reckon.'

Callahan suddenly backhanded the sheriff, rocking him in the saddle. His eyes were blazing as he watched the lawman poke his tongue into the new split in his bottom lip.

'Get goin', Linus!' he gritted. 'I like to see the faces of men I kill.'

'You wouldn't've seen the judge's, holed up on the roof of the ferry shed, away on his left!'

'Christ, you are tired of livin', ain't you?' Callahan spoke through clenched teeth, his eyes cold and without lustre like those of a dead man. 'Now, go get your posse spread out like I told you. No! One more argument, Linus, and I'll blow you clear outta that saddle!'

That was it. Doolin was pigheaded, but he knew he didn't dare cross the line now Callahan had drawn it. He nodded jerkily and without a word, he wheeled his mount and rode after the posse.

Callahan watched him go through squinted eyes, finished his cigarette and then rode back down to the trail leading towards town.

Dakota knew he was in big trouble now.

The grey was weakening from the amount of blood it had lost – and leaving a trail it would take him a week to cover.

He had stopped and wadded a kerchief over the wound. The bullet had passed through a saddle flap before hitting the horse and he jammed in the cloth, arranged his saddlebag on that side so it rested squarely over the bullet hole in the leather, thinking it would help hold the cloth in place.

It worked well enough but it wasn't enough to stop the bleeding. He had come to a small stream, walked the horse into it and washed away the blood from the hide and leg. His own boot and lower trouser leg were sprayed with the animal's blood, too. He stroked the grey's muzzle and spoke quietly to it, grateful it had given him so much. It must be in real pain. He had gingerly felt around for the bullet but it was in too deep for it to bulge the hide and be felt from the outside. That wasn't good.

It might have grazed a lung, judging by the angle it had gone in. Apprehensively, he checked the horse's nostrils and the back of its throat but so far there was no sign of blood coming and the saliva was normal.

He scooped up a handful of mud from the stream bank, wadded it into a flat cake and slapped it over the wound. The horse whinnied and moved away quickly but he kept talking quietly and soothingly, managed to work some of the mud down into the bullet hole. Maybe it wasn't too hygienic, but sometimes mud held curative minerals and, in any case, it would surely help stanch the blood-flow.

He washed the blood-soaked neckerchief, wadded it under the saddle flap again and this time used a rawhide thong taken from his war bag to tie the saddlebag down firmly so that it held the cloth in place.

It was all he could do and he didn't have a lot of faith in it holding but there was a long way to go yet before he reached Cougar Creek.

He just hoped the horse would make it that far.

The girl was anxious to get away and Doc Halloran didn't try to keep her.

'Marv's seriously hurt but he'll pull through, all right. Needs bed rest and daily treatment. You get along about your business, Dianna. You've done your part.'

She hesitated, smiled at the gaunt, grey-faced deputy.

'I have to go, Marv.'

He nodded. 'I know. You hurry, but – stay safe. And I'm obliged for your help, ma'am.'

She unhitched the buckboard and left it and the team in the doctor's open stables, saddled and mounted the buckskin, and rode out of town by the back streets.

She didn't shake Callahan that easily, though. He was watching from a vantage point not far from the doctor's, pursed his lips and decided to let her go.

For now.

He hitched his mount to Halloran's picket fence and walked straight into the infirmary where the doctor was working on the deputy, suturing the wound. Halloran snapped his head up.

'Dammit, Roy, you know better than to barge in here like this! You're bringing all kinds of dirt and germs with you.'

'That right, Doc?' Callahan said casually and walked right up to where the heavily breathing Torres lay on the table, his side exposed and all bloody, half-way stitched up. The gunslinger leaned down for a closer look. 'You do good hemstitchin', Doc. Be a shame to have to rip it out, wouldn't it?'

Torres's eyes flew wide and Halloran straightened indignantly.

'What the devil are you talking about?'

Callahan flapped a hand towards the deputy.

'Need to ask old Marv some questions, Doc. I ain't got a lotta time so I thought if he couldn't gimme the answers I wanted to

119

hear, I could kinda speed things up a little by givin' him a little pain.' He smiled grimly. 'You know pain does wonders for the memory sometimes, Doc. How many stitches you put in there already?'

'Five and I have at least another five to go, so if *you'll* go, I'll get on with it.'

'Told you I need to talk with Marv. Hey, Deputy. Where you say Dakota nailed you?'

'Out – along the trail – in the direction of the pass.'

Callahan shook his head slowly.

'No. He wouldn't head for the pass. Wrong direction for him and wrong answer from you... You know the question, now you just think on it again while I try to jog your memory.'

Torres screamed as Callahan rammed his fingers into the gaping part of the wound and ripped it wide open, the catgut tearing through the reddened flesh.

'Oh, good Lord a'mighty!' thundered Doc Halloran lunging for the gunslinger.

Callahan rammed an elbow into the medic's midriff and stopped the man in his tracks. Torres was writhing, sobbing in pain, blood flooding out of the wound and reddening the sheets. Callahan slapped his face back and forth half a dozen times.

'You gotta pay attention, Marv! I'm gonna ask you one more time. Then mebbe Doc'll have some new wounds to sew up for you. Savvy...?'

Shortly afterwards, Roy Callahan came out of the doctor's house, whistling between his teeth, drying his hands on a small towel which he threw into a drooping flower garden as he walked down the path to where his horse was tethered.

He mounted and left town at a good clip.

He didn't have to worry about talking with the girl now or even trying to follow her. He knew where to go – and what sign to look for.

Splashes of blood if that swing station hand was right in thinking Dakota's mount had been winged.

Callahan smiled to himself. Wouldn't be long before the blood along the trail to Cougar Creek was coming from Dakota himself...

And there would be plenty of it.

The grey was weaving and staggering and Dakota couldn't bring himself to make it work any longer. It had done mighty good, better than mighty good, and he wasn't about to let the animal suffer any longer.

He dismounted on the high, narrow trail, which took a hairpin bend and dropped sharply right on the edge of the ravine, the trail that would lead him on into Cougar Creek country once he had made the descent.

The grey wasn't going to make it: if he tried to ride the wounded animal down there he would be straddling a dead mount before half the distance was covered. The animal was blowing hard now when it breathed and he tightened his lips when he saw the pinkish tinge around the nostrils. The damn bullet had grazed the lung, all right.

Well, it looked like the grey was finished. And he couldn't let it suffer after the valiant effort it had put into bringing him this far. He didn't really want to shoot off a gun but he had to put the animal out of its misery. Dakota had his six-gun out, instinctively checking the loads in the cylinder, when he decided he would use his knife instead.

It was a good knife, honed to a razor's edge, and the point was sharp, the blade seven inches long. If he picked the spot just right he could drive the steel deep into the base of the throat, sever the big artery, and, after a little discomfort, the horse would simply lie down and drift away.

Dakota wasn't a cruel man and some people had noted that he was less cruel to animals than some human beings he had tangled with. He always said that human beings ought to know better than to do some of the god-awful things they did to other humans.

The grey was swaying now, snorting with bubbling sounds, its legs starting to fold. Dakota drew his hunting knife, then his hat was whipped from his head. An instant later he heard the whipcrack of a rifle. He drove backhanded with the knife, burying it to the hilt in the hot, dusty hide. The grey snorted and whinnied, shaking its head, even tried to rear but it was already too weak.

It collapsed slowly, going down to its knees. Dakota kept it between him and the rifleman, thrust hard against the horse, helping to tip it onto its side so its back was facing the shooter. He hunkered down between the twitching legs as a bullet whined off the saddle and another slammed into the quivering animal.

He swore when he realized the horse had fallen on the wrong side: his rifle was beneath the animal now. He only had a six-gun against a rifle and that gave the killer the advantage of range and more stable sighting.

Smoke drifted from up the slope amongst some pale sandstone boulders. It gave Dakota a general direction and as he sighted carefully on it, the rifle cracked again. He reared back as blood and flesh splashed from the horse into his face. He dropped flat as several more shots thudded into the almost dead animal, finishing the job.

He scrubbed a hand hard down his face, spat, rammed his shoulder in close against the grey's belly.

'Too bad I didn't bring the Creedmore, Dakota!' a voice called down mockingly from the boulders. 'But don't worry – I'll nail you good, even if it takes all afternoon! I got plenty of ammo!'

Dakota swore.

Callahan! Damn the son of a bitch! How had he get on my trail so fast...?

The hell with questions, he told himself. Sounded like Callahan was alone, so that was something. He wondered how far away was the rest of the posse...?

Behind him was a drop of a couple of hundred feet into the ravine. He was on a steep sloping part of the trail, using energy just to stay put. He actually felt the dead horse slip a few inches and braced his legs against the grey's forelegs. Two more shots raked the saddle, a third cracked and mangled the stirrup iron where it lay on the rise and swell of the horse's belly.

Pinned down! But no damn use staying put or he was a dead man for sure!

The thing was, what could he do about it?

He didn't know Callahan very well but from what he'd seen he figured the man was impatient – not in general everyday things, but when it came to killing. Once he had decided to kill his man he wanted it over and done with. That talk about taking all afternoon was eyewash. Pretty soon the man would shift position, trying to get a better angle, or he might even stand up...

Even as he had the thought Dakota saw Callahan's shirt as he moved, and he snapped two fast shots. As the six-gun's echoes slapped away across the slope, he heard the last of Callahan's startled curse, saw the man's hat, bullet torn, sliding across the sandstone. *Hell, he had almost nailed him!* He might even have clipped the point of the man's shoulder and then the bullet had gone on to rip the hat from his head.

That must've been al-mighty close!

But he knew it had been plain luck and he

didn't want to count on how much he had left of *that!*

Then Callahan, angry at almost being killed, emptied his rifle down into the horse's body, some of the slugs gouging rock and kicking dust. Dakota lay low, reloading his Colt, and as soon as there was a pause long enough to indicate that the rifle was empty, he jumped up and snapped two fast shots at the boulder, seeing yellowish dust kicked up. He leapt over the horse's forelegs to start down the steep slope, but he became entangled and stumbled.

The movement set the grey's carcass sliding and Dakota was knocked off his feet, sprawling and rolling towards the edge.

Roy Callahan jumped up, only two shells pushed into the rifle's breech now, flung the weapon to his shoulder and fired them so close together there seemed to be only one prolonged explosion.

Dakota weaved but stopped suddenly as if he had hit an invisible wall. He was starting to crumple when the sliding horse's carcass hit him and carried him over the edge into the ravine.

Callahan stared for a dumb moment and then burst into laughter.

'Got him!' he crowed.

CHAPTER 9

DEAD AND GONE

Callahan wanted to make sure.

When he shot a man they stayed shot, but he wanted to see Dakota's body for himself so he climbed down from his high spot and skidded and slid his way down the steep slope where the fugitive had holed up behind his horse.

There was a large blood-slick from where the horse had bled after Dakota had thrust the knife into its throat. This overlaid some of the skid marks left by Dakota's body when he had fallen and rolled towards the edge, knocked over by the massive weight of the sliding horse. Callahan was breathing a little hard through his flaring nostrils as he made his way carefully to the spot where man and animal had gone over. The edge had broken away and the blood-trail ended here. He leaned out gingerly, looking down into the brush-choked ravine bottom where birds were just settling again after the disturbance of the falling bodies crashing into their territory, seemingly out of the sky.

The brush and small saplings had been crushed flat down there and he could see part of the horse, lying crumpled and very dead, half-screened by branches and leaves. He let his squinted gaze wander slowly left, then right, above the grey's carcass and below.

'Where the hell are you?' he said aloud, annoyance in his voice. He grabbed a rock at the edge and leaned out further.

He frowned when he could not see Dakota's body. He saw what he figured was the man's hat caught up in a bush but there was no clashing colour of his shirt amongst the greenery.

'Come *on!* I know I nailed you, you bastard! Where the hell *are* you?'

The anger was overwhelming the good feeling he always experienced after a kill and he grew a little reckless. The killer slipped and he dropped a couple of feet, jarring his boots against a protruding rock, snatching wildly at other rock for a hold. His eyes widened and sweat popped out on his face, his heart slamming against his chest.

Man, that was close! Too damn close!

Callahan dragged himself up onto the

broken edge of the trail, sat there, letting his breathing and heartbeat settle. He had seen something down there, about ten feet below. It looked like a small ledge, hidden from direct view from above by a slight outward bulge of the cliff top. He didn't see how Dakota could possibly have landed there: the way he'd fallen with the horse, he was likely to have gone *out* and away from the narrow ledge, which was further hidden by a line of rocks.

Well, he knew what to do here.

Roy Callahan reached back to where he had laid down his rifle while he took his first look over the edge. He levered in a shell, lay flat on his belly and edged out enough so he could just see the rocks lining the outer part of that ledge. It was awkward and twisted hell out of his big body but he hammered five thundering shots down there, ricocheting them from the outer edge. Only one missed and angled outwards to be lost somewhere in blue space before eventually dropping down into the ravine. The others struck the inward slopes of the rocks, *whanged* across to the back of the ledge or screamed along the floor, ricocheting two or three more times in diminishing speed.

But if anything – any*one* – was lying down

there, they would be slashed to pieces by the flattened, flying bullets. Callahan was chuckling as he edged back, grunting with effort.

'*Adios*, Dakota! You were way outta your depth – but I guess you know that by now!'

He sat with legs dangling over the edge, rolled a cigarette and lit up, raking his gaze around the ravine below in one final sweep. He could ride down that precarious trail, of course, and then find a way through the rocks and batter a path in through the brush, but...

'Hell! He was hit bad and he's dead now!' he snapped in final decision. He stood up, and flicked his cigarette out into space, and climbed slowly back up the steep slope to where his horse was tethered amongst the high rocks.

One thought struck him, though: this trail hadn't been marked on that fake map Bantry had drawn for Dakota – so that meant someone had told him about it.

Likely that damn Darcy woman.

He would have to see about that, but first he would report back to Bantry – and collect the bounty of 1000 bucks that the man had placed on Dakota's head.

Callahan was a man who liked to spend money and to enjoy the pleasures it could buy. The things he was going to do with that $1,000 bounty kept his mind occupied as he rode back through the hills.

He was concentrating so much on this that he failed to see Dianna Darcy way below on a lower trail.

But she saw him.

She had been watching him for the last twenty minutes. The gunfire had attracted her in the first place and she had had trouble finding a way up from the low trail. The buckskin, normally a docile critter, had almost stood on a snake a little while back and, though the reptile had whipped away in fright and hadn't made even a token strike, the horse was now skittish and leery of this country.

It had delayed her reaching the higher trail where all the shooting seemed to be coming from: a rifle and a six-gun, the shots bursting in short volleys. And it had been the rifle that had fired last. She had grown up with guns and been taught their finer points by her father, and she had passed this information on to Chuck as he had grown. So she could tell the difference between the heavier thunder of a rifle and the flatter, shorter crack of a carbine. As there was no carbine being used in the fight she knew the rifle was in the hands of the aggressor and the six-gun being used by Dakota.

Her heart fluttered with worry when the gunfire had ceased, the echoes of the rifle fire dying away. Then, finding a way up the steep trail, she had seen Roy Callahan, rifle in hand, sliding down an even steeper part of the trail, towards the edge where it dropped into the ravine.

She remained hidden, watching him looking down, standing on a freshly broken trail edge. Then he had slipped and for a moment she had hoped he had fallen into the ravine. But he had scrambled back, grabbed his rifle and fired five rapid shots whilst hanging out over the edge.

At first it had puzzled her, then she remembered the narrow ledge hidden from the trail above by the slight outward bulge of the cliff. She only knew about it because she had once tracked a wounded cougar up here. The lion had been ravaging her herds night after night and she had lain in wait, spotted it in the early light just as she was about to give up and triggered as it made a snarling leap towards one of her cows. It spun and corkscrewed in mid-air, screaming in anger and pain. The spoor showed yellow bile mixed with the blood and she knew she had gut-shot the mountain lion.

Her father had always stressed never to abandon a wounded animal, whether it be a deer or high-country sheep, or even a snake.

'If you set out to kill it, then kill it – as quickly and painlessly as you can. No need to let any critter suffer needlessly.'

So she had trailed that mountain lion and it had led her to that narrow ledge. It had been almost dead from the effort of climbing down there when she eventually found it and ended its misery.

When Callahan was well out of sight, she made her way to the broken edge of the steep trail, looked over and saw the carcass of the grey 200 feet below in the crushed brush. She drew in a sharp breath, briefly wondering if Dakota could be trapped beneath the horse. If so, then he was dead and gone...

But she refused to dwell on that aspect. There was the ledge to check out.

She soothed the nervous buckskin, took her lariat and tied it securely around the saddle horn. Then she paid it out as she backed up to the edge, put some weight on the rope and felt the horse take the strain, acting instinctively, for it was a working horse after all. Very carefully, she took the first tentative step over the edge, tested the rope again, but the horse was holding now quite willingly.

Dianna lowered herself down, breath coming in gasps, her heart crashing against her ribs.

'Dakota?' she called tentatively.

No answer.

She called again several times, easing down a little more after each call failed to bring a response. She was really worried now. Because of the deep shadow and the line of bullet-chipped rocks edging the ledge, she couldn't see into it properly. She had come down too far to the right, began to crab-walk across to her left so as to reach the ledge.

Then she saw him. Slumped against rocks on the outer edge, shirt torn and bloody, more blood on the side of the face that she could see, mixed with dirt and ingrained chips of rocks.

He wasn't moving. He looked dead.

Sheriff Linus Doolin spun in the saddle when he heard three rapid shots echoing through the mountains.

His hand dropped to the six-gun butt as he squinted against the afternoon sun, looking up and to his right as three more close-together shots crashed out.

Sounded like one of the boys had found something!

'And about goddamn time!' he gritted. They hadn't found any real sign all day. A few false alarms but nothing they could call a real lead to this damned Dakota.

They ought to have known when he killed those two hardcases sent to nail him after Judge McManus was shot that he was going to be a hard nut to crack. If they could keep him on the run long enough he would be caught – or, preferably, shot to death on sight, even if it was in another state. But Doolin wanted to see the man dead himself – and he could use that extra 1000 bucks bounty, too.

While thinking this he was already spurring his mount through the sparse timber and out on to open slopes where he could see a rider up there on a small bare bench reloading his six-gun.

'Callahan!' he breathed and spurred his weary mount up the grade, seeing other posse men closing in on the point, having heard the signal, too.

The gunslinger was waiting for them, leaning on the saddle-horn, a cigarette curling smoke up past his small eyes as he kept it clamped between his thin lips. There was a smirk on his face as he watched them straggle in.

'What's all the racket?' demanded Doolin irritably. Callahan ignored all questions until most of the posse had arrived.

'Thought you were a long ways from here,' Doolin, tried again.

'Yeah. Been over to the Cougar Creek trail.' Callahan raked his mocking gaze around at the trail-stained, dirty townsmen, tired and saddle-sore from their long day in the wilderness. 'How you boys like to sleep in your own beds tonight? Snuggle up to your wives and girl friends, wake up in the mornin' and go about your regular lives again?'

They looked blankly at him, and as the meaning of his words sank in and the eyes glittered with excitement, Doolin said, face deadpan as usual, showing nothing but scepticism:

'Why would we head back to town so soon?'

'Because I'm tellin' you you can do just that.' Roy paused, making them wait for it. 'I've nailed Dakota. He's dead an' gone! And I claim the bounty!'

That caused a stir and a barrage of questions but Callahan let them all override each other's questions until they quieted down. Then he said:

'Caught up with him on the Cougar Creek trail. His hoss was wounded. I pinned him down and shot him off the goddamn cliff!' He lifted a hand and made a nosediving motion like a hawk swooping on its prey. 'Two hundred feet straight down, the hoss, too – which I think could've landed on top of him – so you could say, Dakota was flat-out dyin' in that ravine!'

No one laughed and Callahan cut his own chuckle short when he saw his joke had failed to amuse.

'You didn't bring back the body?' Doolin asked, face tight and Callahan glared.

'You want to climb down there and scrape him up it's OK by me, Linus.'

Doolin pursed his lips. 'Bantry'll want to see the body.'

'Then *he* can go out and scrape him up. Hell, Dakota's dead, I tell you. When I shoot a man he stays shot. Anyone knows that...'

Doolin scrubbed a hand around his stubbled jaw.

'Yeah, well, you're the one has to tell him. And you want us to call off the hunt, right?'

'Christ, are you dumb? *The man's dead!* You want to stay out here in the dark twiddlin' your thumbs, that's OK by me. But I'm ridin' in to report to Lang. Anyone wants to come along is welcome.'

Of course, the whole posse, including Doolin, followed him down out of the hills and back to Stillwater where they arrived a couple of hours after dark.

Lang Bantry was eating supper in his room. He was accompanied by a rather nice-looking blonde woman who served the courses. She was dressed only in a thin gown over a sheer nightdress and was quite aware of the effect her long legs and jutting bosom had on Doolin and Callahan when they entered.

Bantry looked from their faces to the blonde, caught her amused gaze, and jerked his head towards a door. She set down the coffee pot and slouched away, giving them all an eye-popping view of her swaying buttocks. Callahan whistled softly through his teeth as she closed the door behind her.

'I'll take some of that instead of the bounty on Dakota!' he said.

Bantry paused with the coffee pot poised above his cup, his eyes burning into the gunslinger.

'Shut your mouth, Roy,' Bantry said quietly. He filled his cup. He eased back in his chair after sipping the coffee and finding it too hot. He looked at Doolin. 'I hope that means that Dakota is dead.'

Doolin shrugged, jerked a thumb in Callahan's direction. 'He says he killed him.'

Bantry's cold eyes swung back to the gunfighter. 'Says? You don't have the body to show me?'

'Two hundred feet down a ravine, Lang,' Callahan said confidently. 'My lead in him and possibly a hoss lyin' on top of him.'

'You saw this? You saw his body?'

'Sure. Through the field glasses,' Callahan lied easily.

Bantry frowned. 'If the horse was lying on top of him how did you see him?'

'Arm and a leg stickin' out. He's dead, Lang, take my word for it.'

'Why should I do that, Roy?' Bantry's voice was almost purring and Callahan's face showed he was losing a little confidence now.

Doolin stood to one side, arms folded as he leaned his shoulders on a wall, looking amused.

'You know when I say I shot someone they're dead, Lang. Hell, look at the judge!

One shot in bad light and I nailed him dead centre.'

'Oh, I know the judge is dead, because I saw his body. But I won't know Dakota's dead until I see *his* body.' Bantry leaned forward a little, drilling his gaze into Callahan's face. 'And I don't pay any bounty until I do see Dakota's body.'

'Hell, Lang! It'll take half a day to make our way into that ravine and then we gotta move the hoss and scrape him up–'

'Sooner you start the better, then.'

Callahan blinked. 'You mean – now?'

Bantry spread his hands. 'Sooner you bring me Dakota's body, sooner I pay you the bounty. You go with him, Linus.'

'Aw, now, wait up a minute! I don't get none of this bounty and it means goin' way to hell-an'-gone over to Cougar Creek...'

His voice trailed off under the unwavering, bleak stare and he sighed, nodding.

'OK. But it ain't fair!'

Lang glanced at Callahan. 'How'd you know to head over to Cougar Creek?'

Callahan told him, relishing the details of how he had made Marv Torres talk about the swing station and the wounding of Dakota's horse.

'He must've got that from the girl,' he

finished. 'And she must've told him how to find the right trail. He couldn't've done it from that map you gave him.'

Bantry stood. 'I'm impressed, Roy. You've used your head. Now you go bring me Dakota's body and then we'll arrange some kind of accident for Diana Darcy – and maybe Torres won't recover from his wounds, either.'

'You better go easy with the Darcy gal, Lang,' warned Doolin worriedly. 'You know how the town feels about her.'

'Anyone can have a fatal accident, Linus. Anyone at all... Good evening, gents. And I don't expect to be disturbed before morning – for any reason.'

He said this last flatly, nodded curtly, then walked towards the door the woman had gone through.

CHAPTER 10

GUNSLINGER'S BLUES

It wasn't the easiest job getting Dakota off the ledge and up to the trail.

Dianna had been surprised to find he was still alive. The wound in his head had apparently come from striking his skull on the rock edging of the ledge. Two bullets, flattened from the opposite wall, had slashed across his back, one at the shoulders, the other just above waist-level. Incredibly, they had only barely broken the skin, just enough to make it bleed, and then had splattered against the rock. His lower back was peppered with small dots of blood from the fragments of the shattering lead bullets.

It seemed that another slug had torn the heel off one of his boots and then buried itself in a patch of clay on the ledge. But when she rolled him over she found a wound in his chest. Not actually in his chest, but through it. Or at least through the muscles. It had apparently struck him while one arm was raised, punched through the chest muscle and out again without doing a lot of damage. Mind, the chest muscle was torn and he would feel it for a few weeks, but it was on the left side and likely wouldn't slow him in any way that really mattered.

'You ride with Lady Luck for a saddle-mate, Dakota,' she said aloud, although he was still unconscious from the blow on the head.

There was a good deal of blood but a lot of it was smeared so she reckoned he hadn't lost too much.

The ledge was stinking with old manure and the remains of meals eaten by the cougar that had once inhabited it. She looped the rope around the unconscious Dakota, under his arms, strained and scrabbled about as she pushed some of the edging rocks over the side and watched them bounce a little way before dropping through space to the brush near the grey's carcass 200 feet below. She ran a tongue across her lips, wishing she hadn't watched those rocks fall. It was too easy to replace them with images of herself falling, in her mind...

She jumped when Dakota suddenly groaned but his eyes remained closed. Still, he must be getting close to coming round, she decided. She eased herself to the cleared edge, and, holding the rope above Dakota's body, used her weight to drag him to the very lip of the ledge. She had to lean out into space to do this and gritted her teeth, willing herself not to look down.

Dianna searched and found a place where there was solid footing. She swung Dakota's body past the point of balance. She cried out in fright as he seemed to drop, but it was only the slack in the rope, freeing itself from where it had looped around a rock. He swung in space, head hanging loosely, and she fought to grab the rope and stop the pendulum effect. It almost pulled her off her feet, but she regained balance, snatched at a protruding rock and then called to the buckskin above.

'Buck! Back up, boy! *Back! Back, boy!*'

Nothing happened and she swore mildly: the damn horse would pick this time to play stubborn! She called again – and again – and just as she was about ready to start climbing up there herself, the rope moved. It slid upwards and Dakota's slowly turning body rose a foot, then two feet. He banged against the cliff face a few times but not very hard. It was unavoidable anyway as his body continued to rise, inch by inch.

Then the horse stopped of its own accord and she swore again, but immediately relented. The horse could have backed up against the brush or a tree, in which case he would stop until commanded to move or coaxed around it. She tried calling without success and then knew there was nothing else for it.

She would have to climb up and try to manage the manoeuvre from above.

There were several handholds, at least two just beyond the reach of her straining arms, but she inched her way across until she could grab them, then heaved with her trembling, aching legs, gaining another foot in height. Dakota was starting to come round, his body twisting at the end of the rope. She knew it was likely the pain of the rope itself cutting into his wounded chest that was making him stir and she wondered what damage it was causing.

But there was nothing she could do about that right now. It was essential she got him up onto solid ground as soon as possible. She rested, breathing hard, feeling dizzy, hearing her blood pounding in her veins, face pressed against the rough surface of the cliff. Then she drove herself on and up, arms trembling, legs quivery, wondering if she was going to have any strength left by the time she did reach the top.

Suddenly she was sprawled across the broken edge, one knee grinding painfully into the crumbled rock. She moved the leg, got a hold with her boot and pushed hard, thrusting up onto the trail, grabbing for whatever handhold she could find.

As she lay there a moment, getting her breath, she found herself looking at the rope where it ran across the broken edge. She froze, the panic starting to swirl within her.

The sharp edge of the shattered rock had cut into at least a couple of feet of the rope as it passed across, fraying the plaited strands. As it rested there now, moving and creaking with the motion of Dakota's swaying body, strand after strand was wearing through. She imagined she could hear the minute poppings as they snapped one by one.

Dianna wrenched her head around, saw she had been right, the buckskin had backed up against the timber. She got to her feet, staggered to the horse, patted its muzzle, spoke gaspingly but soothingly to it, and then manoeuvred it away from the tree.

'Back up, boy. That's a good horse. Backup – *Back!* Good! Good! Keep going...'

The horse was moving at an angle now and she ran to the edge, threw herself flat and saw the rope sliding across the broken edge, the jagged rock sawing away at the strands. It was not only rising now, but moving sideways at the same time because of the buckskin's angle.

Which meant it was being worn through at twice the rate as previously...

With a small cry, she tore off her hat and, as the rope moved across, held the thick felt just underneath where it was standing away from the cliff edge. Then, jamming it there, hoping the rope wouldn't dislodge it, she sat up, reached between her feet as she rammed her boots against solid rock and grabbed the rope with aching, torn fingers. She strained with the horse and as the rope slid up she heaved sideways, using her full weight to pull it across the hat.

She smelled the pungent odour of burning felt as the lariat slid across and stopped moving in a sideways motion, but continued to ride upwards, Dakota's body rising slowly.

'Hey! Wha – what's happening?'

She jumped at the sound of his voice calling from below the edge, leaned down and smiled through the dirt on her face.

'You'll be safe in another few minutes. If you can, help by using your feet to give a little purchase...'

His efforts were feeble enough but in three minutes he was sprawled, groaning and gasping, on the trail and she stopped the horse.

Dakota grunted in pain as she unknotted the rope and pulled it from around his torso. There was fresh blood from the bullet wound soaking his torn shirt.

'Just – let me – get my – breath,' she said, 'and I'll – bandage those wounds. Are you feeling much pain?'

'Felt – worse. Not much, mind. Thought I was gone. Callahan shot me over the edge and the grey slid down on top of me. Glimpsed a ledge and tried for it but – don't recollect reaching it.'

'You did – and you were lucky. Callahan must've seen it and fired down into it, ricocheting his bullets. A couple cut your back but not too deeply...'

'I'm – mighty obliged – Dianna.'

'Don't thank me yet. We've a lot to do and a long way to go. We'll have to ride double for one thing...'

It took a good deal of time. But she had had the forethought to pack one of Chuck's shirts and a small flask of brandy in her saddlebags. By the time she had finished working on his wounds Dakota had emptied the flask and claimed he was feeling a heap better.

'I think that's the spirits talking,' she told him, smiling slowly. 'The chest wound is nothing more than a hole drilled through the muscle – which will be plenty sore enough, I should think. But that gash in your head is quite deep and probably should be stitched. It hasn't stopped bleeding entirely yet. Will you be able to sit up behind me on the buckskin?'

'If he don't mind, I don't.'

She looked at him sharply. 'Maybe I shouldn't have given you all that brandy. You can't be feeling all that good.'

'Lady, three years in Stone Dog teaches you just how much pain you can stand. If you can't make it, too bad. They dump you in an unmarked grave. It's a damned good incentive for *making* you endure things you never thought you could, would or should ever have to...'

Dianna was sober now. 'It must've been – terrible.' When he said nothing, she added slowly, 'I think I begin to see just why you agreed to take that shot at Judge McManus.

You must have hated him terribly.'

'He wasn't my favourite person. But there's no time to waste on stewing about hatred in a place like Stone Dog. You learn to push it to the back of your mind and sometimes you can bring it out and look at it during the night, but mostly it just stays there – while you dream about the day you'll get even. Never really believing it'll ever come.'

'But your day came last Sunday...'

'Too good a chance to pass up. But folk will never believe I didn't kill McManus.'

'Unless you can get Bantry to admit he arranged the whole thing...'

Despite his wounds and the pain, Dakota managed a weak smile.

'That won't be an easy thing to do – but it's the *only* thing that'll clear me.'

'You ... you'll still go after him, even when you recover?'

'Hell, yeah. I won't get far long as that "shoot on sight" tag is there.'

She had been thinking while she prepared the buckskin for the long ride back to Stillwater. Now she turned towards him.

'There's a US marshal in Wichita Falls. Suppose we sent him a wire, arranged a meeting where you could explain what happened?'

'Whoa! I'm wanted for escaping prison as well as everything else. I don't reckon any lawman's gonna give me much chance to explain. Won't believe me, not with my background.'

'But it's a better chance than trying to get to Bantry and make him talk. You have to have someone in authority to hear him confess! A US marshal's perfect, Dakota.'

He knew her reasoning was OK but he just naturally shied away from confronting a lawman: he had had too many bad run-ins with them over the years.

Anyway, he could think about it some more on the ride back to town.

Sitting the saddle was a strain but Dakota was tough and ground his teeth to avoid moaning in her ear every couple of minutes as she guided the buckskin down the slope.

They were heading back towards the Stillwater trail when he said suddenly:

'I don't want to go back to town.'

She snapped her head around but couldn't see him properly as he was too close, actually holding her waist.

'We could stop at the ranch overnight but you really should see about that head wound!'

152

'It'll be all right. The bleeding's slowing. I've got a headache but I'll be all right. I don't want to go anywhere near Doolin and Callahan. I'll try to get away through Cougar Creek, rest up some and then maybe come back and straighten things out.'

'"Maybe"?'

'Yeah. I'm tossing up whether to risk my neck by trying to clear my name of this murder or make a run down into Mexico.'

She gasped. 'I – I didn't think you'd give up like that.'

'I'm one man, Dianna. Bantry has a big organization. I'm not boasting when I say I'm pretty good with guns, but I've got a feeling I'm running out of luck. Anyway, I've never been to Mexico.'

'You told me once you always pay your debts.'

'I will, but I can wait.'

'You could never return here even if you made it.'

She sounded dull, disappointed, but she could also see how it made sense in one way. He had been on the run from one thing or another for a good part of his life. His one attempt to settle down and make a go of things didn't work out and now he had been framed for a murder he would have hell's own time trying to break free of.

'Think a little more about it, Dakota, please. I think that marshal would be sympathetic. I know him slightly and he seems a fair man.'

'How about the wire? Bantry runs Stillwater. I guess that might include the telegraph office.'

She was silent for a short time and then said:

'I never thought of that, but I'm afraid you're right. Manny Cartwright, the telegraph operator, is one of Bantry's men. He lets him see everything that crosses his desk.'

'There you are, then. Let's go to Cougar Creek.'

'But – there might be a way!' she said excitedly. 'Doc Halloran has no love for Bantry. I'm sure he would agree to transfer Marv Torres to Wichita Falls for more treatment of his wounds. We could smuggle a message to the marshal with Marv. I'm sure he'd do it. He's beholden to you for taking him to the stage station...'

'Yeah, but I'd still have to meet that marshal and my feeling is he'd want to lock me up till he checked around at least and–'

He got no further.

A rifle crashed and a bullet passed in front of Dakota's face, close enough to tug at the girl's hair. She gasped and he started back, tightening his hold on her waist instinctively.

A voice called from the darkening trail up the slope and slightly to one side.

'Now ain't it lucky Lang made me come back to check that I'd really killed you, Dakota! By Godfrey, you got more lives than a charmed cat! But they all end right here!'

And Callahan triggered the rifle again just as Dakota threw his weight against the startled girl and knocked her from the saddle. He started to fall himself and had enough presence of mind to snatch the rifle scabbard, gripping it tightly with both hands, dropping his full weight on it.

The rawhide thongs holding it to the saddle flaps snapped and he carried the rifle with him as he jarred against the hard ground. The startled buckskin ran off.

The girl was still rolling downhill but managed to slow her progress, spin her body around and crawl swiftly in behind a rock. She heard Callahan curse and then a bullet whined off the rock. She ducked, trying to see Dakota.

She didn't know how he had done it but

he was crouched behind a deadfall and even as she watched he swung his right arm violently out to the side. Dianna blinked as the saddle scabbard came loose from the rifle and then he was levering in a shell, rising to one knee, gun to shoulder.

He fired four fast, raking shots and she distinctly heard Roy Callahan cry out in alarm. But he wasn't hit, or, leastways, not badly, for his gun opened up and splinters were chewed by the handful from the deadfall sheltering Dakota.

The outlaw was sprawled flat and she could hear his ragged breathing. Then she saw him moving, moving along the length of the deadfall, working his way in amongst the sprouting, earth-choked roots at one end. Callahan fired again but his bullets still hit in the area where Dakota had been originally.

He didn't know Dakota was in the tree's root system.

'The girl's dead, too, Dakota!' Callahan called with a vicious note in his voice. 'I can see part of her amongst the rocks and I'm gonna put one into her hip, smash it up, drive the bone splinters into her, cause her a lot of pain. Unless you want to step out and take it like a man. What about it, killer?'

'I say go to hell, Callahan!'

The girl blinked. She felt sick at his words, not game to move because there simply was no way she could use the rocks to hide her body any more than they did already.

Then Callahan laughed.

'Hell, it don't matter! I got a hankerin' to maim her anyway. Never liked her. Nor her kid brother. Soooooo...'

While he was talking he swung his rifle towards the girl's hiding place – and exposed his right side to Dakota, not yet realizing the man had changed position.

Dakota whipped the rifle to his shoulder and triggered. Roy Callahan was blown off his feet by the strike of lead. He crashed down off his rock to land amongst some brush.

Dakota was already clambering up the slope, staggering with fatigue and effort but moving in on the killer. He stepped amongst the rocks and saw Roy struggling to get up, his right side all bloody, the ends of two shattered ribs poking out through the flesh and the torn shirt. His face was very white in the half-light and his eyes widened when he saw Dakota. His right hand flashed back to the butt of his Colt.

It must have cost him plenty to make that

move but it did him no good. His hand was already slippery with blood and the gun fell from his grasp.

Dakota held his rifle low, the butt braced into his hip. Callahan glared his hatred through the pain in his squinted eyes.

'I – still got – another – gun...' he gritted and fumbled his left hand for the Colt holstered on that side.

Dakota shook his head slowly and fired, levered again, fired a second time.

This time when the bullets smashed him down, Callahan didn't move at all.

CHAPTER 11

MESSENGER

Mexico was out.

Dakota knew it as he sat with his shoulders pressed against the deadfall, gasping for breath, blood trickling down his face from under the improvised bandage the girl had covered it with. He had jarred his body hard when he had spilled from the saddle and he felt like he was the lone survivor of a stampede that had passed through the trail camp.

Dianna knelt beside him and eased up one side of the bandage. She winced.

'The wound has opened up. You'll need stitches. You could have some internal head damage, too.'

'Figure I've had that ever since I listened to Lang Bantry,' he murmured. 'But after three years in Stone Dog, a man'd make a deal with the Devil himself.'

She smiled slowly, shook her head a little as she moistened the bandage with some water from the canteen.

'You're a tough man, Dakota, but you'll never make Mexico in this condition.'

He surprised her by nodding gently.

'I know. I guess we better go to your ranch.'

'That's fine, except I can't tend that head wound. I've stitched up gashes and cuts but this is a sort of punctured wound and I think I can see some bone. You need a doctor.'

He swore and didn't even apologize. She squeezed his hand.

'At least you'll have a horse of your own now.'

She meant Callahan's mount, of course.

'And a couple of six-guns and his rifle,' he added, ever the practical man of violence. 'OK – we stop at your ranch but leave in time so we get to town just before daylight.'

She agreed. 'One thing: town's the last place they'll look for you.'

'Yeah. That's a bonus. Getting out again might not be so easy though.'

'Give some more thought to having that marshal come down. And what about – Callahan?'

He looked at her steadily. 'He's the one killed Chuck, isn't he?'

160

She flushed. 'Yes, but – these hills are full of wild animals.'

'He won't know.'

'You're not only tough, Dakota – you're hard!'

'When you're dead, you're dead. But you go ahead and cover him with some rocks if you want. Just take his gun belt and six-guns first – and I could use a new pair of shoes and a hat...'

She hesitated, then nodded gently.

'Yes – I'll do that.'

He closed his eyes.

'Call me when we're ready to leave.'

Sheriff Linus Doolin thought: 'To hell with it!' and banged a fist on the hotel room door several times.

He waited, running a tongue around dry lips, wondering if he was being stupid doing this. After all, it was barely daylight...

The door opened and the tall blonde woman he had seen in Bantry's suite last night stood there, holding a thin robe together with one hand. There was still a lot of her pink curves to be seen but Doolin looked into her mocking face.

'I need to see Lang.'

She pushed some strands of golden hair

off her face, the gesture somehow disturbing Doolin. She smiled a little.

'He's sleeping.' She yawned for effect. 'We were both tired. Very tired.'

Her innuendo made the sheriff mad.

'Go wake him up and tell him I'm here.'

'You *sure* you want me to wake him...?'

'Aaaah!' Doolin shouldered her aside impatiently and strode through the small parlour to the bedroom door which was ajar. He stopped dead when he saw Bantry was propped up on one elbow, the sheets having slipped, showing he was naked – at least from the waist up.

'What the hell d'you want so goddamn early?' he demanded thickly, scrubbing a hand through his tousled hair.

'Good mornin' to you, too, Lang.' Doolin stepped in and closed the door. He thought he heard the blonde, who was almost at his heels, say a cuss word. 'Roy ain't back yet.'

Lang Bantry frowned. 'Back...? Oh, yes. I sent him to bring me in Dakota's body. He said it was in a ravine. Probably hard work getting it out.'

'If it was there.'

Bantry's eyes narrowed. 'What?'

'Roy told me he wasn't sure he was down in a ravine. There was a small ledge but he

162

didn't think Dakota could've reached it. He emptied a rifle into it to be sure, ricochetin' his bullets...'

Bantry was sitting up straight now, the sheets across his thighs. Doolin noted with one part of his mind that the man was entirely naked.

'So he lied to me. When he gets back you send him to me right away.'

'Was wonderin' if I should send someone lookin' for him, Lang. That Dakota's a slippery one.'

Bantry frowned. 'You think he may still be alive and he ... got Callahan?'

'We-ell, Roy's the best, I guess, but he ought've been back by now. It's no skin off my nose if he's lyin' out there with a bullet in him, but I want to see Dakota dead as much as you do.'

'Then you go look for Roy.'

Doolin blinked. 'My deputy's still poorly at the sawbones. Won't be easy gettin' a townsman to go with me.'

Bantry shrugged. 'Your problem. Just remember, the more men who are in on the kill, the more to split the bounty with.'

Doolin scowled: even half-awake, that damn Bantry knew how the wind blew.

Dakota felt better after a rest in a decent bunk at Dianna's ranch but he was still stiff and aching and his head throbbed. Now and again he felt dizzy but he tried to hide this from the girl.

She made an early breakfast which they ate by the light of the fire in the pot-belly stove which was used for cooking as well as winter heating. They left soon after. Dakota rode with Callahan's rifle across his thighs, constantly looking around at the countryside as it gradually took form in the strengthening light.

It was still very early when they reached Stillwater. Only a few people were about, mostly down at the river, fishing or tending skiffs. As far as he could make out, no one saw them enter town and ride along a backtrail to the doctor's place. The yard had only been fenced by strung wire and several lengths of this sagged almost to the ground, low enough so they didn't have to use the ricketty gate. The horses simply stepped over the limp wire. They ground hitched the animals and Dakota had to reach out quickly to the wall to steady himself. The girl was at his side in a flash. She took his arm and helped him to Doc Halloran's back door.

Inside, Halloran told them that Torres was making progress but would need bed rest for some time yet. The ribs were his biggest problem, he said as he tended to Dakota's head wound, cleaning it out thoroughly.

'Nasty bang you've had here, Dakota. Exposed the bone but it's not fractured, luckily. You're going to have a headache for a few days and maybe your vision will be affected but it will be only temporary. I'll stitch it now.' He glanced at Dianna. 'Perhaps you'd like to go and see Marv?' He smiled crookedly. 'Dakota's liable to do a little cussing once I start.'

She left and the sawbones was right: Dakota writhed and cussed a blue streak and told the doctor when he had finished that the wound didn't feel any damn better.

'Worse if anything!'

Halloran smiled wearily. 'It will give you gyp for a day or two. But you did right by coming to see me. Left unattended it might've turned septic and eventually you'd have died of blood poisoning.'

It still didn't make Dakota feel any better.

They went in to see Torres who was looking pretty good but still very tired and drawn.

'I spoke to Marv about Wichita Falls,' the

girl told Dakota right away. 'He's agreed to carry a message to the marshal.'

Doctor Halloran frowned.

'Marshal Dobbs? Am I missing something here?'

Dianna explained, Dakota staying silent. When she had finished, Halloran nodded slowly.

'Yes, it sounds like a good idea. Actually, Marv could benefit from seeing the thoracic surgeon there. They have a decent hospital and I am a little worried about those splintered ribs.'

'Whatever you say, Doc.' Torres looked at Dakota. 'Be glad to help you out after what you done for me.'

'I did it *to* you,' Dakota pointed out quietly, squinting some from the pain in his head. Adhesive plaster held a pad over the wound.

'But I wouldn't be alive now if you hadn't taken me to that stage station. You can wrap your message in oilskin and cover it with my bandages in case Doolin or someone gets the idea of searchin' me...'

The girl noticed Dakota's face and said:

'Dakota isn't keen to face the marshal. He thinks he'll lock him up until he investigates.'

166

'I don't doubt he will,' Halloran said. 'But at least you'll be safe in a cell, Dakota.'

'Doc, I've had three years of cells and holes in the ground. I've no hankering to spend any more time in them.'

'Well, what's the alternative, boy? Stay on the run? Never being able to relax, never knowing when a bounty hunter's bullet is going to find you?'

'All right! I'll see this Dobbs. But he's not going to lock me up anywhere. I'll kill him if he tries.'

The room fell silent, all three watching him.

No one doubted that he meant it.

'You can stay here,' Halloran offered and when Dakota agreed, the medic said, 'You'd better get Callahan's horse under shelter in my stables.'

'I'll do it,' Dianna said heading for the door.

The doctor packed a pipe and Torres and Dakota rolled cigarettes. But before any of them had lit up, the girl came bursting back into the room, white-faced.

'Roy's horse has gone! You couldn't have ground-hitched him properly, Dakota!'

'Damn!' said Torres. 'He's likely to wander up town.'

Roy Callahan's horse was unmistakable. It was a high-shouldered black with the top of its right ear missing. This had been chewed off long ago by a wild dog in a desert crossing Callahan had been making in an effort to escape the vengeance of three brothers and the father of a gun-happy kid he had killed in a badlands town a week earlier.

Doolin recognized the black as soon as he saw it while he was saddling his own mount in the small brush-roofed stables behind the law office and jail. He stopped what he was doing and ran across the yard to the gate in the fence. The black was drinking at the small stream outside the yard and looked up casually as the sheriff approached.

Doolin was a familiar figure and the black waited for him, did not object when the lawman took hold of the bridle and spoke quietly. The sheriff stroked the muzzle and kept hold of the reins while he examined the animal closely.

Then he led it into the yard, tethered it in the stable with his own mounts and hurried to Lang Bantry's suite of rooms in the hotel.

'No signs of blood, Lang,' he reported, 'but he's come a long ways. Got some bluish clay on his legs and we only get that out

168

towards Cougar Creek. Rifle's gone from the scabbard and Roy's spare shirt is missin'. There's only one box of shells left, too, and he always carried three or four.'

'And what do you conclude from all this, Linus?' Bantry asked unsmilingly. He had dismissed the blonde woman as soon as Doolin came in and his mood had darkened since the sheriff had started speaking.

'Well ... looks to me like mebbe Roy fell off or was shot outta the saddle, but he was only wounded.'

'Why? You said there was no blood.'

'No. But he could've fallen quickly so it didn't splash on the saddle or the horse.'

'And he could've been killed with a single shot.'

Doolin moved his feet uncomfortably.

'Mebbe. But the boxes of bullets missin' makes me think he put up some sort of fight.'

'And...?'

'Well ... he got killed or was too weak to get back on the hoss and it just wandered on back to town.'

'Or, whoever killed him caught the horse and rode it back.'

Doolin stiffened. 'Aw, I dunno about that, Lang.'

169

'Roy said Dakota's horse went into the ravine. He was sure he'd killed the son of a bitch but to me it sounds like he hadn't and Dakota ambushed him, took his horse.'

'Judas priest! You mean – *he* might've rode Roy's black into town?'

'It's possible and if there's a chance Dakota's here, I want the bastard's hide nailed to the wall! You get searching. Right now!'

Doolin frowned. 'No deputies, Lang, and I know there ain't any townsmen want to go nosin' around lookin' for someone like Dakota! It's too close here in town for their likin', I reckon.'

'Christ, man, what am I paying you for? Get a couple of hardcases and pay 'em twenty bucks apiece – dangle the bounty in front of 'em. You'll get some help that way.'

But Doolin still wanted that bounty for himself.

'What about them two fellers you use as bodyguards? Gann and Burdin?' He didn't think Bantry would pay them any bounty: they were on his payroll and well paid already.

'They'll be staying close to me as soon as I send for them,' Bantry said flatly. 'You find your own men and do it *now!* I want this town searched from top to bottom, every alley, every backyard shed and lean-to, every house and store...'

'Hell, there's gonna be some fuss about that!'

Bantry glared at Doolin bleakly, saying nothing.

The sheriff hurried out, muttering, figuring maybe Gil and Turk Parsons would be the ones to approach. He'd had them in the cells and once on the local chaingang for rolling drunks. He was sure they'd killed a few Indian bucks who'd run from the reservation. They were always broke.

Best of all they were dumb: violent and cunning and ruthless, but dumb. No one would miss them if they were shot down while trying to bring Dakota to heel. That way *he'd* be the only one to claim the bounty. He smiled thinly to himself as he hurried around to the back of the saloon where the Parsons had a smelly lean-to they used for sleeping off their drunks while in town.

As he went he sniffed and felt his nostrils rasp and twitch. There was a brown smudge cloaking the hills and he swore.

There was a dust storm moving in on Stillwater.

CHAPTER 12

DUST TO DUST

They didn't want Dakota to go but he wouldn't listen to them, checked his six-gun, collected the rifle that had belonged to Callahan, and went out through the rear door of the doctor's house.

If the horse had wandered off, it was his fault. They couldn't deny that but nor could they convince him that it was too late for it to matter – whose fault it was, that was. By now the horse could have been seen.

'So I'll go make sure,' Dakota told them.

'This is ridiculous!' snapped Dianna. 'I can do it with a lot less risk!'

Torres and the doctor also argued but by then Dakota had checked his weapons and was gone.

His head worried him some, the blinding headaches. They were affecting his vision a little, in flashes, but it seemed to be a dull day and he was grateful for that. Sun-glare wouldn't have helped. He was surprised when he glanced up and saw the writhing smudge over the hills. He had seen enough dust storms in his life to recognize one closing in on the town. He hurried along the back lanes, catching a glimpse of the black's sign here and there. It was making for the stream, which he had figured would be its destination, anyway.

There were three kids playing there with wooden boats, wading out knee-deep. They stared at him as he came towards them, eyeing his rifle a little apprehensively.

'Seen a black horse wearing a saddle?'

They didn't answer at first and then the freckled one with tousled red hair said in a piping voice, pointing towards town proper:

'Sheriff was leadin' a hoss like that a little while ago.'

'Thanks, kid.'

'Can we have a look at your Winchester?'

'Some other time.'

'Aw, come on. We helped you!'

'Some other time, kid.'

As he turned back quickly towards Doc Halloran's all three boys put their thumbs to their noses and waggled their fingers. They were fighting a sea battle, arguing over who was going to be John Paul Jones, when two scruffy-looking men came out of one of the streets that led up to Main.

They were rough and unshaven and one had a shotgun in his hands. One of the boys, who had turned from the sea battle to blow his nose through his fingers, saw them first. He nudged the others and all three stiffened.

'Gawd! It's the Parsons!' whispered the redhead.

'Hey, you kids! You see anyone around? Big *hombre*, square jaw, dark hair. Might be wounded...'

Gil asked the question. He was the elder brother, wore a heavy stubble that wasn't yet quite a beard. He had a hooded lid at the corner of his left eye.

'Dunno. Might've.' Again it was the red-haired one who spoke up. 'It worth a quarter?'

Turk, thinner than Gil but with the same lopsided cast of features, lifted the shotgun. 'Worth a bellyful of buckshot to try dickerin' with us?' he countered.

All three of the boys suddenly felt an urgent need to urinate and moved closer together. They all knew Turk Parsons' reputation.

The one who had blown his nose began to sniffle and the third boy's bony knees knocked together. The redhead looked pale,

175

his freckles standing out. His thin arm shook as he pointed.

'Went back that way.'

Gil nodded, tossed a coin towards them. It splashed into the muddy water but they were too scared to go plunging after it, just stared as the Parsons moved away in the general direction of Doc Halloran's and other houses that backed onto the small stream.

'You'll have to hide,' Dianna said, face taut, after Dakota told them what the boys had said. She glanced at the sawbones. 'Doctor...?'

He frowned. 'My wife is an invalid. You could hide in her room. Under the bed, perhaps... I believe I could head off any search by showing my indignation...'

That didn't appeal to Dakota but Torres spoke up:

'Can't fight 'em here, Dakota. Gunshots'll bring 'em all down on you.'

Dakota nodded: he didn't want to bring trouble down on Halloran anyway.

So the doctor hurried him upstairs and into the dim room where Mrs Halloran lay abed, apparently sleeping. The room smelled stale and of sickness and Dakota grimaced as he slid under the bed, clutching his rifle. It clanged dully against a chamber pot.

He swore softly as the door closed after Halloran.

The Parsons arrived not long after, shouldering roughly past the doctor when he opened the door to their thunderous knocking.

'Will you stop that confounded noise! I have a sick wife upstairs who has just gotten off to sleep and–'

'Where is he, Doc?' demanded Gil as Turk went poking his nose into rooms, shotgun cocked.

'Who? What're you doing, breaking in here like a couple of robbers...?'

Gil pushed his six-gun muzzle up under the sawbones' wrinkled jawline.

'I'm a deputy now, Doc. Lookin' for Dakota. We found the hoss he used out back. We know he come here.'

'Don't be absurd. The only visitor I've had all morning is Dianna Darcy. She rode in to visit Marv Torres. And lucky she did, because I have to transfer Marv to Wichita Falls. He's poorly and needs better attention than I can give him. Look, do what you have to, but just don't wake my wife. I have to prepare Marv for his journey and the stage will be here soon.'

The Parsons clumped through the place like a troop of soldiers and Halloran accompanied them to his wife's room. She was still sleeping, but made a slight sound and started to turn. The doctor hustled the Parsons out, his face angry.

'By heavens, if you two wake her up...!'

'All right, all right, Doc!' Gill growled. He spat on the hail floor. 'Goddamn room stinks anyway!'

They interrogated Dianna briefly, glared at Torres as he lay, apparently only semi-conscious, and then, muttering, left.

Halloran's hand was shaking as he wiped his kerchief over his sweating face.

'Mean and terrible men, those.'

Dianna's stomach was only now settling, too.

'I'll write out the message to the marshal if you'll get Marv ready, Doctor. We haven't much time before the stage arrives. It usually only stops for a change of horses before tackling the hills.'

'Dust might delay it, but you're right – we can't waste time. You can tell Dakota he can come out now.'

Dakota came out of his own accord, glad

to be clear of that room. He hoped he would never be that old and ailing that he would end his days in such a fashion. Hell, he *wouldn't*. If he lived long enough to start fading away and losing his faculties, he'd go out and challenge the fastest gun alive.

That way would be quick and final. And it would be his choice alone.

But he was a long way from being ready to go just yet!

'Goddamnit! If the girl was there it's likely Dakota was somewhere around, too!' raged Doolin when Gil Parsons reported they had searched the town without success but that the kids had definitely seen Dakota in the vicinity of Doc Halloran's. 'Roy'd seen her headin' for the Cougar Creek trail.'

Gil shuffled his feet. 'Well, Turk's watchin' the place, Linus.'

Doolin's eyebrows shot up in surprise at this demonstration of intelligence. He hadn't figured the Parsons could think for themselves.

'He's in the trees behind the sawbones'. We got to thinkin' how Doc hustled us outta his wife's room. Mind, I was glad to go. Place stinks. We din' get a chance to look around in there so we thought we better play it safe...'

'All right. Well, I better come with you and we'll search the other part of town, too.' Doolin peered out of a grimy window. 'Dust is gettin' thicker. Stage is gonna be late.'

'Aw, yeah. Forgot. Doc's sendin' Marv Torres to Wichita Falls. He ain't doin' so good, it seems.'

Doolin spun around as he reached down a rifle from the rack.

'He was OK when I seen him last. Halloran said a few days abed and he'd be all right...'

'Must've took a turn for the worse. That Darcy gal was s'posed to be lendin' a hand.'

Doolin frowned. 'Ye-ah. Sounds OK, but I got me a hunch there's somethin' more behind it. C'mon. We'll go to where Turk is. Seems to me Halloran's is the place to be right now.'

'Aw, I was hopin' to have time to slip into the bar. I'm dry an' gonna get a helluva lot drier with this dust storm comin' in...'

'Let's go,' Doolin said, moving swiftly to the door. 'And forget drinkin' till we find Dakota and nail him.'

'Well, it's a long shot, you ask me...'

And hard on Gil's words came the dull but unmistakable roar of a shotgun.

From the rear edge of town.

There was no argument this time. Dakota simply turned on his heel as Halloran prepared Torres for the stagecoach ride, and Dianna sat at the table in the parlour, writing swiftly as she set down the details for the US marshal in Wichita Falls.

They both looked up sharply and the girl called his name but Dakota was already out through the rear door. She dropped the pen and ran to the window. He was running across the yard.

And then he disappeared as a swirl of thick dust passed between him and the house.

'Perhaps the dust will be an ally,' Halloran said quietly from the doorway. 'Let me light a lamp for you, girl. It's getting dark in here.'

Dianna nodded. She thought that maybe the medic was right: the dust might give Dakota cover and allow him to take her horse and clear town.

That wasn't Dakota's plan. He passed the horse still ground-hitched behind the doctor's house and ran for the back way along the stream again. *He* had thought of using the dust storm, too. Instead of running again, he figured maybe he could use its cover to get to Doolin, or even Lang Bantry himself and put an end to this once and for all.

Have one or both of them ready to talk by the time this Marshal Dobbs arrived in Stillwater.

That was his plan, but Turk Parsons had other ideas.

Grit crunched between his rotten teeth and rasped at his nose as he waited in the dimness of the trees. He tugged his hatbrim lower so as to protect his eyes a little and then rested the shotgun's butt on the ground, the barrels against the tree, while he pulled his neckerchief up over his lower face. He had just got it into place when he saw Dakota leave the house.

Turk snatched up the shotgun and lifted it to his shoulder, ready to blow Dakota off his feet. Then a wall of heavy dust blew between him and his target. He started to cuss, then figured: *why wait?* He'd had Dakota beaded. The man couldn't move *that* fast!

So he squeezed the trigger; a second later he pulled the other one. The shotgun bucked and rocked his body again. The thunder of the shots was distorted by the eddying dust clouds as he broke open the gun, pulled out the used shells and thumbed home two fresh ones.

With a little luck, he wouldn't need them. But Turk's luck was not running for him that day.

Dakota tripped in the murk the instant the Greener's first shot blasted. As he sprawled he heard the whistling of the buckshot charge passing overhead. Instinct kept him rolling swiftly to one side and the second charge tore up the ground around him, one ball stinging his upper arm.

He kept rolling, twisting his body so that he moved towards the trees and the little stream.

Dust stung his eyes and made him choke, but he saw the movement at the edge of the trees over there as Turk Parsons hurriedly reloaded.

Dakota spun onto his belly, brought up the rifle and put two quick shots into the man. Parsons slammed sideways against the tree, sobbing, wrenched around so his shoulders pressed against the rough bark, and brought up the shotgun, jerking the triggers as Dakota shot him through the heart.

The Greener leapt from Parsons' hands and he dropped to his knees, fell awkwardly sideways, legs tangled beneath him. Dakota thumbed home three shells into the smoking breech and plunged across, hammer back. But Turk was all through. Dakota knelt and set down his rifle. He grabbed the Greener and felt in the dead man's pockets for shells. He found three, put two into the shotgun, the third in his shirt pocket.

He heard pounding boots coming, splashes as someone ran across the shallow part of the stream a little way down. He couldn't see anything. The dust wall was locking-in on the town now, choking it off from the rest of the world.

A rifle and six-gun hammered and bullets flew wild around him, chewing bark from the trees, cutting small branches, raining leaves and twigs down upon him. Gripping the shotgun, he rolled away, forced to abandon his rifle now. He wrenched around and saw two hazy forms coming towards him.

He fired at one, heard a man yell and sob in agony, then there was only one form coming at him, but the man's rifle or carbine was hammering, the butt placed against the man's hip, lever and trigger working as fast as Doolin could manage.

Dakota wrenched his head aside instinctively as he felt the wind of a slug past his face. He lost balance and the shotgun went off, shooting wild, wasting the charge of buckshot. Still, although it was wild, two balls took Doolin in the right arm and forced him to drop his rifle.

Cursing, he wrenched at his six-gun, running forward all the time. Dakota was just getting up when the man cannoned into him, dust stinging their eyes as they groped to grip each other, falling together.

Doolin tried to club with his six-gun. Dakota butted him in the face, feeling the nose crunch and the splash of warm blood on his forehead. The sheriff's legs wobbled and Dakota dug in his boots – Callahan's boots, to be accurate – and rammed a shoulder into the lawman's midriff.

The impact lifted Doolin off the ground and Dakota kept charging forward, an arm around the man's waist, trying to slam him into a tree. The sheriff pounded Dakota's bent back, grunted as he jarred against a tree. But he wasn't square-on and Dakota stumbled as they slid around the trunk. Doolin lifted a knee, three times – *bam! bam! bam!* – into Dakota, knocking him sprawling and writhing. The outlaw hugged his mid-section and Doolin came in, boots swinging.

One caught Dakota on the upper left arm and he felt it go numb clear down to his fingertips. Another boot caught him in the side and he almost passed out, feebly

185

grabbing at Doolin's leg. He hugged it to him like a long-lost child and when Doolin, cursing, moved and tried to shake him, he went with the motions.

Doolin stumbled, off balance with the extra weight while Dakota tried to get air into his lungs and fight the pain in his damaged ribs. Doolin bared his teeth in a snarl, twisted fingers in Dakota's hair, and wrenched his head back. He clubbed a blow downwards, fist like a hammer as it sought to smash Dakota's nose clear out of the back of his head.

It hurt like hell, but Dakota threw himself sideways, feeling hair literally tear out of his scalp. The blow took him on the shoulder, half-way between neck and tip. It rocked him, drove him down, and Doolin tried to lift a boot into his face.

Dakota, instead of grabbing it this time, rammed a hand up into the man's genital area, clutched and twisted savagely. Doolin screamed and writhed, pounding frantically at Dakota, missing more blows than he landed.

It was an uneven battle.

The sheriff collapsed and Dakota got out from under him, releasing his hold, throwing the man onto his back. He straddled him and began pounding on his jaw, blow after blow, smashing the man's head from side to side on the ground which he could barely see now in the choking, blinding dust storm.

His throat was full of grit, his saliva turned to mud. His eyes were sticky and raspy, his nostrils clogged. He eased back long enough to pull his neckerchief up over his nose and mouth, twisted up the front of the dazed lawman's torn and bloody shirt and raised a fist for another blow.

'What the hell's all the shootin'?' bellowed a voice suddenly and several others demanded an answer to the same question.

He squinted, holding the blow. Shadowy forms were splashing across the stream – he could just hear the sounds over the roaring and rasping of the dust storm in his ears.

Someone yelled and there was a bigger splash as he fell.

'Hell! There's a dead man's legs trailin' in the water! One of the Parsons...!'

'Doolin deputized 'em earlier! They're huntin' that Dakota.'

'Judas! Is he in town! See you later, fellers!'

'Me, too!'

'Fools! He's worth a thousand bucks...'

'Well, what're we standin' here for? Let's get after the son of a bitch!'

Dakota rolled away from Doolin, groped around and found the shotgun. He would rather it had been Doolin's rifle, but there was no time now.

He had to get out of here: half the blamed town was going to be looking for him now!

CHAPTER 13

DEAD END

Bantry looked at Doolin's obvious injuries and the painful way the man walked but there was no trace of sympathy in his eyes. He curled a lip.

'You let him get the better of you – again.'

'Hell, can't see a damn thing in this dust, Lang! I literally fell over the top of the sonuver. He nailed Turk and Gil and damn near finished me. I was lucky the townsmen showed up when they did.'

'You told me they wouldn't want to search for Dakota!'

'We-ell. They'd been drinkin'. Might as well use 'em, Lang. They can flush Dakota for us.'

'For *you*, Linus. This is your job.'

Doolin eased a hip gingerly onto a corner of the desk.

'Hell, Lang! I've already lost two men, had my nose broke, my balls turned to mush! I can't do it alone!'

'I don't care how you do it, Linus. Just do it.'

'I seen Gann and Burdin hangin' round downstairs. Can't I borrow them? I need someone fast with a gun, not these half-drunk bakers and storekeepers. Christ, they'll be shootin' each other in that stinkin' murk out there...'

'Gann and Burdin stay here. You're beginning to bother me, Linus. Once I could give you a chore and know it'd be done. But since this Dakota arrived, you've been a pain in the ass. Excuses for this and that–'

'Wasn't me let Dakota get outta that freighter's room in the first place,' Doolin said sullenly.

'It was you recommended the men who were supposed to kill him,' Bantry said very quietly.

'Well, it was them let us both down. Lang, I dunno where I'm at. Takin' orders from Callahan, runnin' all over the countryside, drunks stumbling round town in a dust storm. Hell, I don't even know why the judge had to be killed!'

Bantry stood, leaned his knuckles on the desktop, boring that frosty gaze into the sheriff.

'Because the stupid bastard was so dazzled

when they asked him to run for governor, he signed an undertaking for land reform! You know what that'd do to me? Ruin me overnight! They'd take everything I have and throw me in jail. McManus hid that deal from me so – he had to go. As long as there was no suspicion thrown on me, Dakota was the perfect choice.'

'Mebbe you might think twice about that now,' Doolin said quietly and winced at the look on Bantry's face.

'Don't come to me again, Linus, unless it's to report Dakota's death. Now, *get out!*'

Doolin flinched and stood up hurriedly, limped towards the door. 'Send Gann and Burdin up here, too,' Bantry snapped, mouth tight in fury.

A couple of minutes later there was a knock on the door of Bantry's suite and his two bodyguards came in, Gann and Burdin.

Gann was the taller, not bad-looking, clean-shaven, neatly dressed – Bantry insisted that they wear clean good quality clothes, but he made them pay for them out of their salary. He wore only one gun and the holster, although oiled, showed sign of long wear and use. He favoured tight leather gloves and he tugged these now as he look at his boss.

Burdin was thicker through the body and came only to Gann's shoulder. He sported sideburns and a thin, straight moustache with the suggestion of the miniature goatee on a lantern jaw. His hands were big and he didn't wear gloves, but, like Gann, carried only one six-gun. There was a .44 calibre derringer in a special small holster inside his wide trousers' belt for back-up but he seldom needed it.

When these men went out to kill, one shot from their pistols was usually enough. Neither was very good with a rifle, though, but, at the same time, each had bushwhacked men with long-arms when ordered.

'You know Dakota's on the loose,' Bantry told them without preamble. 'I want one of you downstairs, the other outside this door. Night and day, until he's dead.'

'Long hours, Mr Bantry,' Gann said and didn't flinch from the killer stare.

'You'll be paid accordingly. It may be all over by sundown. If we can tell when that is, with all this damn dust about. You know Dakota. You see him or even anyone you think might be him, shoot to kill.'

Burdin looked sharply at Gann and the taller man pursed his lips.

'That could cause some trouble if it turns

out to be a townsman.'

'Worry about that later.'

And Gann showed a slight surprise as he realized that for the first time in the three years he had worked for Bantry – beating up cowhands working for spreads the man coveted, killing occasionally, even breaking into government offices to get legal documents – this was the first time he had ever seen his employer so worried.

No. It was more than that.

Lang Bantry was actually afraid.

And so he ought to be.

For Dakota had made up his mind now: he wasn't going to run any more. He was taking the initiative. The odds were not in his favour but, hell, when had they ever been? It had always been rough and he had always had to outrun pursuit for one reason or another.

He was a man who attracted trouble wherever he went and he had always ended up facing it squarely, even after a long flight.

Now this had come down to the same point: it was time to put his back to the wall and fight like hell. Make a last stand if that was the way it was going to go, but *fight!*

Only this time he figured: why wait for

them to come to him? He knew Bantry was in town. Sure, he had Gann and Burdin to protect him – Dakota had met them before they set him up for the McManus killing. He hadn't been unduly impressed but he knew such men and he was wary: they would not be easy to get by but he would find a way.

The main trouble was to get back into the town proper. These half-drunken townsmen were raging through the dust storm in the back streets and he heard gunfire at random intervals as they shot at anything they thought was moving and looked like a man.

He had heard two men cry out in sudden fright and pain: it wouldn't be long before a townsman was killed – by one of his so-called friends.

The dust was still thick and turning day into night, helping him in one way, hindering in another. It covered his movements, but he couldn't see through it any better than the drunks and he could well be shot down in one of their wild volleys. Now that would hurt! Being killed by a bunch of drunks.

He figured he was down behind the saloon on Main now. There were two on Main and two more on side streets. This one he figured was the Hot Spot. Dakota groped his way along the side of the building in an alley strewn with rubbish. He tripped over an abandoned crate and bottles rattled. He froze.

Then he dropped flat as he caught a movement against a lighter break in the rolling dust clouds at the street end of the alley. A rifle cracked and a bullet tore splinters from the saloon wall. The man was panicked and working lever and trigger wildly, shooting all over the alley. Dakota figured it wouldn't be long before one of the stray slugs found him and he snapped a shot with his six-gun. He heard the startled man yell, the rifle clatter to the ground, as the would-be bounty hunter retreated fast around the saloon.

Dakota jumped up and ran back down the alley as he heard men shouting, asking who was doing the shooting and why. They would be surging into the alley any moment.

He cannoned into the wall, stumbled over more trash in the saloon yard. A door opened and someone lunged at him, swinging some kind of club or a length of timber. Dakota leapt to one side and as the weapon whistled past his head, smashed the shotgun's long barrels into the man. His arm jarred and the attacker folded.

Dakota leapt over him. A gun hammered

behind as someone else came out of the door. He hit the wire fence and somersaulted, a starburst behind his eyes as he spilled and kept rolling. He held tightly to the Greener: it had only one shell in it but it could have a devastating effect and would be his best deterrent if he ran into a bunch of these loco wolves prowling the town.

Men were shouting behind him, an occasional gun going off. His neckerchief slipped down over his chin and he sneezed and choked on dust that was flung against him like shovelfuls of dirt. Left was the way he wanted to go but it would take him closer to the pursuers. So he swung right, crashed into a fence post and was knocked to the ground. Just as well, because someone cut loose with a shotgun and he heard two charges of buckshot whistle over head.

'I reckon that nailed him!' a slurred voice yelled.

Dakota bellied under the fence, hauled himself erect and crouched double as he swerved left, figuring the group of men would be angled away from him now as they searched for his body, the shotgun man still boasting that he had brought down Dakota and would now claim the bounty.

He managed to get away from that

particular bunch of hunters and, going in the direction he wanted now, he was forced to veer away when he heard another group coming down from Main, attracted by the shotgun blasts.

He groped and stumbled his way around and when he stopped to try to get his bearings, was astonished to find that he was in the back yard of the law offices.

There was someone in the stables saddling a mount.

It was Linus Doolin, but Dakota didn't know that at first. The sheriff had decided that the best – and safest – way he could carry out his search was on horseback. All these other fools were afoot and a horse would find its way around better by its animal instincts, anyway.

But he heard Dakota as he floundered once again in the murk, knocking a couple of rusty kerosene cans together as he eased through long grass. Doolin dropped to one knee, palming up his six-gun, glimpsing the long Greener and knowing that the gods had smiled on him: they had brought Dakota to him.

But he made a mess of things.

Startled and flooded with a surge of bitter, overwhelming hatred, he couldn't prevent himself from gritting his teeth and crying out Dakota's name.

'Dakota! You're *dead!*'

He triggered hard on the last word but Dakota's reactions were way faster than Doolin realized. He dropped as soon as he heard his name and the three bullets that Doolin fired passed over his head. The fugitive spun onto his back, the shotgun angling across his chest and upwards as Doolin's hate drove him to run forward, still shooting.

The Greener thundered and Doolin stopped dead for a fraction of a second, then was lifted off his feet and flung backwards a couple of yards by the charge of buckshot. Dakota jettisoned the now useless Greener and rolled to one knee, sweeping his six-gun from the holster, hammer back and ready to fall.

No need. Doolin was never going to move again of his own accord. The buckshot had torn his chest open and shattered half his face. The horse had panicked and run off, the saddle sliding around under its belly as it disappeared into the heavy dust cloud.

Dakota didn't waste time. There would be a crowd here any time now.

What was more, now that he was moving out of the cluttered yard of the law office, he had his bearings.

He knew he could find his way to Bantry's hotel without trouble from here on in.

He made the short journey without undue stumbling or taking wrong turnings, but there was trouble awaiting him.

Burdin was just inside the foyer, watching from behind the half-glass doors, much more comfortable than if he had stationed himself on the hotel's porch.

He saw Dakota's crouching figure as the man weaved across this side of the street and felt his way along the boardwalk with his feet, making unerringly for the hotel. Actually, Burdin wasn't certain-sure it was Dakota, but he figured there was a good chance it was.

So he opened one of the half-glass doors, stepped out and began shooting through the murk. One of the bullets was mighty close and Dakota lunged into the street, rolling up to one knee, snapping two fast shots at Burdin's squat form. The bodyguard reeled and flung his gun arm wide. It smashed through the glass panel and Burdin fell head first into it, jagged glass slashing deep into his throat.

Dakota ran along the walk, saw the

dangling body, the man clawing futilely and desperately at the gaping wound as his carotid artery hosed blood into the foyer. Dakota dodged the red jet and ran across the dim room, tearing down his dust-clogged neckerchief, blinking his sore eyes.

Gann appeared at the head of the stairs, a sawn-off shotgun grasped in his hands. He raised the weapon and part of the banister exploded into whirling splinters as Dakota dropped flat. The second charge chewed a large hunk out of the step two above his head and then he was leaping up the stairs with his long legs as Gann whipped out his Colt and started shooting.

Dakota's gun was quicker and Gann was already hurled upright by the outlaw's lead before his gun hammer dropped for the first time. He dropped his gun and grabbed at his belly, one arm hooked around the banister, head sagging.

Dakota leapt onto the landing, looking down into Gann's pain-filled eyes. He loosened the man's arm without effort and shoved, the gunman tumbling and bouncing down the stairs to sprawl in an unmoving heap at the bottom.

'Get out of my way,' Dakota said and ran for the door to Bantry's suite. He kicked it open and went in in a headlong dive for the floor.

Bantry was waiting, his gun blazing.

Dakota rolled and spun, but checked as he lifted his thumb from the gun hammer, holding his fire.

Bantry was standing across the room, a smoking gun in his right hand, his left arm encircling the slim waist of the tall blonde woman as she struggled, her face contorted in fear. But she was an effective shield and Bantry managed a smile as he covered Dakota.

'Yes! I was right! You do have a chivalrous streak in you! A man who shoots another and then shows enough concern and remorse to come back and take him to where he can get help, just *has* to balk at shooting a woman down in cold blood – particularly one as beautiful as Sonia here.' He laughed and raised the gun. 'Well, your chivalry has cost you your life, Dakota!'

'Doolin's dead,' Dakota snapped, disconcerting Bantry for a moment.

But then the room shook to the thunder of a six-gun. The blonde jerked and screamed as she tumbled from Bantry's shocked grip, exposing him. His gun went off but Dakota's bullets stitched a ragged line across the man's chest, twisting him, hurling his body across the desk. He clawed frantically as he sagged back, pulling papers and ink wells and a humidor with him. He sprawled on his back, eyes wide and staring.

Dakota stood, reloading the smoking pistol. He reached down for the wounded blonde and pulled her to her feet. She was holding her upper left thigh which was spurting blood.

'Sorry. But I couldn't let the sonuver win.' She gave him a twisted smile.

'You didn't win, either,' she gasped. 'You just killed the last man who could clear your name!'

Dakota turned from the window in Doc Halloran's and looked at the pale-faced Dianna Darcy.

'Dust is clearing.'

She nodded, looking towards the surgery where Doc Halloran was stitching the wound in Sonia's thigh.

'She's right, you know, Dakota. There's no one who can clear your name now. They're all dead.'

He sighed. 'I thought maybe she might know something but I guess no judge is gonna take the word of a whore without further proof.'

'What will you do now?' Dianna asked quietly.

'Nothing I can do, except make a run for Mexico.'

She frowned. 'You said you've never been there. You don't know the way.'

'South. I'll hit the border eventually.'

'But there are patrols. They'll be watching for you.'

'I'll dodge 'em.'

She was silent for a time and then said, quietly:

'Chuck stocked our land with Mexican cattle. He rode with a bunch of hardcase young cowboys he knew. They raided one of the big Spanish *ranchos*, came back with enough cattle to get our herd started.'

'I hear a lot of Texans got started that way.'

'Yes. I know which trails he used, because he drew a map so he wouldn't forget in case we needed more cows sometime.'

'Can I see the map?'

'I'll do better than that. I'll show you the way.'

He snapped his head up. 'No. Too risky. If I was caught you would be, too.'

'We won't be caught if we stick to these hidden trails – and I know the best places to cross the border and miss the patrols.'

There was rising excitement in her voice now and he stared hard at her.

'Can't let you do it, Dianna. There's your ranch.'

'What's left of it after Bantry got through squeezing me into a corner. It'll be months, maybe years, before it's all sorted out legally in the courts.'

'Well, you'll get it back eventually...'

'No, I'm going to make a new start. In Mexico. With you.'

'Woman, that's crazy! You'll never be able to come back to the States!'

'Nor will you.'

'That's different.'

'Well, I don't care whether I can come back or not. As long as I'm where you are, Dakota.'

He stared at her a long time and neither heard the doctor say that Sonia would be all right and he would be making coffee in a few minutes time ... if anyone was interested.

Then Dakota smiled as she stepped towards him. First they gripped hands, then he folded her in his arms. Doc Halloran shook his head slowly and left the room, muttering:

'Hell, they aren't interested in coffee!'

The publishers hope that this book has given you enjoyable reading. Large Print Books are especially designed to be as easy to see and hold as possible. If you wish a complete list of our books please ask at your local library or write directly to:

Dales Large Print Books
Magna House, Long Preston,
Skipton, North Yorkshire.
BD23 4ND